MYS
HENRY

Henry, Sue,
  1940-

The tooth of time.

| DATE | | |
|---|---|---|
| | | |
| | | |
| | | |
| | | |
| | | |
| | | |
| | | |
| | | |
| | | |
| | | |
| | | |
| | | |
| | | |

8-06

# THE
# TOOTH
# OF TIME

# THE TOOTH OF TIME

## A MAXIE AND STRETCH MYSTERY

## SUE HENRY

 NEW AMERICAN LIBRARY

New American Library
Published by New American Library, a division of
Penguin Group (USA) Inc., 375 Hudson Street, New York, New York 10014, USA
Penguin Group (Canada), 90 Eglinton Avenue East, Suite 700, Toronto, Ontario
M4P 2Y3, Canada (a division of Pearson Penguin Canada Inc.) • Penguin Books Ltd., 80
Strand, London WC2R 0RL, England • Penguin Ireland, 25 St. Stephen's Green, Dublin
2, Ireland (a division of Penguin Books Ltd.) • Penguin Group (Australia), 250
Camberwell Road, Camberwell, Victoria 3124, Australia (a division of Pearson Australia
Group Pty. Ltd.) • Penguin Books India Pvt. Ltd., 11 Community Centre, Panchsheel
Park, New Delhi - 110 017, India • Penguin Group (NZ), cnr Airborne and Rosedale
Roads, Albany, Auckland 1310, New Zealand (a division of Pearson New Zealand Ltd.) •
Penguin Books (South Africa) (Pty.) Ltd., 24 Sturdee Avenue, Rosebank,
Johannesburg 2196, South Africa

Penguin Books Ltd., Registered Offices: 80 Strand, London WC2R 0RL, England

First published by New American Library, a division of Penguin Group (USA) Inc.

First Printing, April 2006
10  9  8  7  6  5  4  3  2  1

 REGISTERED TRADEMARK—MARCA REGISTRADA

LIBRARY OF CONGRESS CATALOGING-IN-PUBLICATION DATA
Henry, Sue, 1940–
The tooth of time : a Maxie and Stretch mystery / Sue Henry.
p.  cm.
ISBN 0-451-21765-9
1. Women detectives—New Mexico—Fiction.   2. Taos (N.M.)—Fiction.   3. Women
dog owners—Fiction.   4. Women travelers—Fiction.   I. Title.
PS3558.E534T66 2006
813'.54—dc22        2005029701

Printed in the United States of America

# ACKNOWLEDGMENTS

**Grateful thanks to:**

Kris Illenberger, Regional Manager, Western National Parks Association, for assistance and information concerning Great Sand Dunes National Park, Colorado—including that handful of sand in the mail.

Pat Dozier, Mary Ann Baron, Kelly Rosenboom, Bettye Sullivan, Alex George Sullivan, and everyone at Weaving Southwest, Taos, New Mexico, who patiently provided a wealth of friendship, information, and hospitality during my visits to this artistic and friendly "town" and allowed me to use Weaving Southwest as a base for the setting of this tale.

Jackie and Al Gamauf, of the Taos Valley RV Park, who provided space to park, information, and permission to wander freely through the grounds, and graciously answered all my questions.

Vickie Jensen and Becky Lundqvist, for their friendship, great senses of humor, patience, and pleasant company on research trips to New Mexico.

And, as always, to my son, Eric, of Art Forge Unlimited, for the maps and photographs.

*For Vickie Jensen,*
*talented writer and photographer,*
*great friend and fellow traveler.*
*Hugs, Vickie.*
*Where next?*

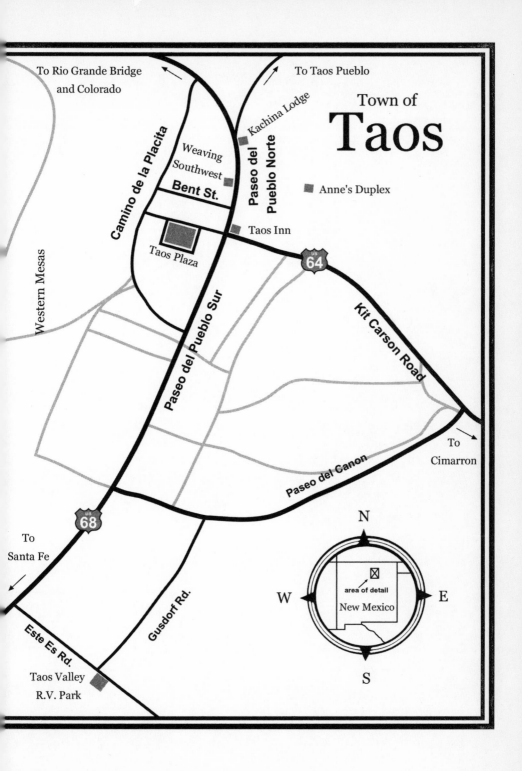

# ONE

*On an otherwise empty westward-tending dirt road, the small cloud of dust raised by a slow-moving thirty-foot Winnebago motor home was gently carried aside by the whisper of a breeze that wandered from a broad meadow between the road and a long, high ridge to the north, an arm of the Cimarron Range of the New Mexican Sangre de Cristo Mountains. In mid-May, the meadow grass was a soft yellow green, in contrast to the dark bluish hues of piñon pine and juniper that began at the foot of the mountains. High overhead a hawk that had nested in the rocky cliffs of the ridge was drawing slow circles against the bright blue of the sky, watching for some small mammal, a squirrel or perhaps a jackrabbit incautious enough to reveal itself.*

*At a spot wide enough to allow a turnaround, the driver of the motor home pulled over and stopped beside the road. After a brief pause, the door to the coach swung open, steps extended, and a woman stepped out with a camera in one hand, the end of a leash in the other. Encouraging a russet-colored mini-dachshund to follow her, she closed the door, turned, and stood facing the hills,* recognizing what she had come out of her way to find and until then had seen only in pictures—a pale arrowhead-shaped peak that rose commandingly midway along the ridge.

Without taking her eyes from the peak, she reached to lay her camera on the doorstep, deciding there would be time for pictures later, when the sun was low enough in the west to add definitive shadows to the ridge. Leaning back against the side of the Winnebago, she slipped the leash around her wrist and pushed both hands into the pockets of her denim skirt, concentrating on the scene before her.

Medium slim of build and of average height, she was an attractive woman, though pretty was not a word that would apply. Handsome suited her better—and, perhaps, interesting—for there was a sharp intelligence in her hazel eyes and a thoughtful alertness about her that would offer the observant the impression that she would probably notice more than the obvious of whatever, or whoever, she encountered. The lines of her face hinted at an approach to life that was more positive than negative, leavened with a well-established sense of humor.

Reaching up, she removed a clip that held her silvering dark hair in a twist, allowing it to fall to her shoulders, and ran a hand through its crown to push it away from her face, still gazing upward at the sharp peak.

"The Tooth of Time," she said softly as if to name it aloud made it more real, thinking that it was different than she had imagined it. But in an odd way it seemed to sum up a lot of what she had experienced in the preceding weeks. "I hadn't expected that."

At the sound of her low voice, more cello than violin in tone, the dog at her feet cocked his head to give her an inquisitive look.

"Yes, lovie," she said, turning her attention to him. "Your walk *comes now. Then, since we have the rest of the afternoon, I think I'll do a little journal keeping. Maybe I can make more sense of it all on paper than in my head."*

*Half an hour later the two were back inside the motor home with the screen door and windows open to the soft breeze. The woman was seated at the dinette table with a glass of iced tea, her journal, and a favorite pen in front of her, the dog napping on a rug nearby. For a few minutes, as she clipped her hair back into its usual twist, she stared out the window at the peak on the ridge, eyes narrowed in thought. Then she opened the journal and began to write.*

Saturday, May 22

Time and age both have teeth—or at least one tooth, if the name of the peak is any indication. Whoever labeled it the Tooth of Time was no spring chicken. It must have been someone on the downhill side of a life, someone who knew what they were talking about and—to totally jumble metaphors—named it with a rueful sense of the shrinking size of their singular piece of the pie . . .

*Through the long afternoon she continued to write, periodically getting up to refresh her glass of tea—once to make a small lunch, which she ate sandwich in one hand, pen in the other, brushing a few crumbs from the page as she continued to record her thoughts in the journal.*

Things that affect you strongly often creep up almost without your realizing, very like the way time passes. The older you get the faster years go by, and then—quite suddenly—you realize that there are less than half of them left. That recognition has an unexpected bite.

I wonder why many people are so desperately afraid of growing old. Some give up and become immediately what they fear most. Others pretend to be younger, generally deceiving no one but themselves, or, just as foolishly, refuse to admit it makes a difference.

I'm glad that, as a senior citizen, I made up my mind to take what comes along as practically as possible, somewhere in between. One of the best things I've ever done was get myself a Minnie Winnie and go off to see parts of the world I had never had a chance to visit, especially doing it on my own, with Stretch for company. But how many people said, "Oh, you can't do that alone, can you?" as if I were too old, or as if being a woman made it something unimaginable and frightening. Most depressing was that most of the ones who questioned my intentions *were* women. I have found that I love to be on the road to someplace new, seeing things and meeting all kinds of people as I come to them. If nothing else it keeps me feeling, if not young, then definitely not yet old.

There are women who, left alone by death or divorce, are terrified to live without a man to take care of them. Being a self-sufficient sort, with or without a partner, I have never felt a need to be similarly dependent. I was very lucky, twice, and will always miss the companionship I shared with both my husbands, that infinitely valuable physical and emotional warmth that was a dependable part of our lives. But it does not fill me with any more anxiety to be by myself in my later years than it did almost half a century ago, before I married either of them.

What happened in Taos was totally unnecessary—and sad. Somehow I still feel I should have seen it coming, though I didn't know the woman and her particular circumstances until it was too late.

To even try to get it in perspective I must think back to where it all began—that, and what happened after I decided to go back to Taos, New Mexico, from the Great Sand Dunes National Monument, after I had spent the better part of two days traveling and trying to convince myself that I had left for good. I'll start again—first to those two days and making up my mind to go back that stormy day at the dunes, then from the beginning—the day I first arrived in Taos, and what came during and after . . .

# Two

You simply never know where chance will take you when you journey as randomly as I sometimes like to do, with no particular destination, or whom you will meet along the way who will change your outlook on—well, all kinds of things, sometimes for better, other times for worse. Considering the usual mix of good and not so good, at least this kind of travel is seldom boring, though it is often not what you expected it to be.

Having spent the greater part of my life as a resident of Homer, Alaska, I've found my later years to be passages of discovery that have turned me into an enthusiastic, motor-homing, senior gypsy, always curious to see what I will come across next. What I found on that particular day in May in southern Colorado was the spectacular landscape of the Great Sand Dunes National Monument.

Nothing could have prepared me for the size of the dune field, or the dunes themselves. I was astonished and awed to find that over time the prevailing wind has deposited some fifty square miles of sand at the base of the Sangre de Cristo Mountains—enough to swallow downtown Denver, tall buildings and all. Constantly changing as the wind moves and sculpts them, at more than seven hundred feet above the San Luis Valley floor the Great Sand Dunes are the tallest in North America. I felt as though I had been transported to somewhere in the Sahara and that a caravan of camels would not seem out of place.

It was late in the day. We had walked a long way over the light and shadow of the enormous dunes and, lost in thought, I had neglected to notice that Stretch was beginning to tire of laboring through piles of sand that were both unfamiliar and often less than stable for a low-slung mini-dachshund of short-legged build. Starting down the lee side of a medium-sized dune, I suddenly felt an unexpected tug on the leash and turned to find that he had finally decided enough was enough and was sitting stubbornly down on the steep slope to await my attention. It was abundantly clear that he intended to remind me there were two of us on this walk and I had better keep in mind that he was the smaller and had been extremely patient thus far, but had not set out to walk off the gloomy mood that, to his disadvantage, I was attempting to alleviate with exercise. I couldn't help smiling, for as he looked at me, head cocked questioningly to one side, both he and the tawny sand on which he rested, exceeding the angle of repose, were slowly sliding toward me and the bottom of the dune.

"Ah, you're tuckered, aren't you? I'm sorry," I told him, feeling contrite. As he slid within reach, I gathered him up under one arm and started back toward the now far-out-of-sight Pinyon Flats Campground, where I had parked my Winnebago motor home before tramping off to experience the dunes. A bundle of energy, Stretch usually disdains to be carried and immediately wriggles to be put down, but on this particular occasion he snuggled against me willingly and tried to tuck his nose under my wrist, then sneezed, twice.

When I had begun this expedition, for well over a mile I had followed a hiking trail north from the campground, crossed a small creek, and come to a picnic area. From there, fording larger Medano Creek required removing my shoes and, with Stretch under my arm, wading ankle-deep through the cold snowmelt from the surrounding peaks.

I had then headed out across the dunes in a northwesterly direction with a pleasant following breeze at my back. Upon turning, I found that in concentrating on the troubles of the past three weeks I had not noticed that what had been a light wind was now more forcefully blowing toward the Sangre de Cristos. It was strong enough to gather up grains of sand and carry them above the surface of each dune, casting them over the edge of the steep face, almost like spray from an ocean wave. The sharp sting of the airborne grains with which that sly wind was now peppering my face, ankles, and arms was downright irritating, to say the least, enlightening me as to why Stretch was attempting to bury his face beneath my wrist.

Nevertheless, to return to my house on wheels I would have to travel into the wind, so I encouraged him to continue his disappearing act and began to make what speed I could in the direction of Medano Creek, the hiking trail, and, ultimately, the campground. I had assumed that, if necessary, it would be easy to find my way back by following my own footprints in the sand, but now they were rapidly being cleverly erased by the wind, which deposited sand into each vanishing depression. The farther I went, the less distinct they became. This was not a particular problem, for though I could not see it over the crests of the dunes that rolled away into the distance, one after the other, like waves on a sandy sea, I knew approximately where my rig was parked, a bit north of the national monument's visitor center.

Abandoning the fading line of meandering prints made earlier, I struck out as directly as possible, given the rise and fall of the terrain, toward the campground. It was slow going through the sand, up and over each dune. The wind whined as I walked and the flying grains became even more abrasively annoying. Stretch whimpered. I swore and wished I hadn't, as opening my mouth allowed in a bit of sand that gritted between my teeth. The sunlight suddenly departed and a shadow swept over us. I looked up to find that more than half the sky was filled with billowing dark clouds heavy with rapidly approaching rain that would undoubtedly begin to fall before I could reach the Winnebago.

If you are outside alone in an unfamiliar place, the moan of a sharp wind sweeping in with bad weather on its back can be disquieting, even haunting. It seems somehow to hold something unfriendly and ominous that encourages seeking whatever shelter is available and leaving it to complain in solitude across wide-open spaces. When you had expected balmier conditions in late May and hoped to enjoy the area in sunshine to counteract a lingering sense of anger and disappointment over events of the previous weeks, the gathering signs of an approaching storm are even less welcome.

The clouds continued to roll in from the southwest. Lightning flashed in the distance, thunder growled, and the wind was now a constant ululation. I was thankful to crest the last dune, plunge down it to cross the creek, put my shoes back on, and hurry south on a more direct gravel road, ignoring the hiking trail. By the time I reached the campground I could see people scurrying about to collect or fasten down any loose items around their tents, campers, and motor homes that the impudent wind could snatch and gleefully carry off. The first fat drops splashed down around me as I passed the nearest tent. They rapidly increased to a wind-whipped downpour and in seconds both Stretch and I were soaked to dripping.

Reaching the motor home at a trot, I fumbled my keys from a pocket, unlocked the door to the coach, and clambered inside, in one motion setting Stretch down and reaching for a hand towel from the galley to stanch the water streaming from my face and hair. He hesitated only momentarily, then shook vigorously to rid himself of rain and sand—adding to what I had carried in—and padded off to take a long drink from his water bowl.

It was dark enough to switch on a light as I shed my wet clothing and finished toweling myself off before donning a dry pair of sweatpants and a favorite yellow sweater so well worn that its cotton fabric felt soft and soothing. Filling a cup with water and adding a teabag, I set the microwave for a couple minutes and left it to do its thing while I brushed the sand out of my hair and fastened it into the twist that I clip high on the back of my head to keep it off my neck. Adding milk and sugar to the tea, I settled comfortably at the dinette table to sip it while I listened—a bit smugly, I admit—to the wind's vexation at our escape. I could feel the motor home shudder as it was buffeted with rhythmic gusts and hear the fingers of rain tapping disapproval on the roof overhead.

Weary Stretch curled up in his under-the-table basket and went to sleep.

I considered taking a nap myself, but knew I had too much on my mind and would just toss and turn on my bed in the back of the bus until I had come to some kind of decision concerning the threats I had run away from in Taos the day before.

The unconscious gist of that thought stopped me. Interesting choice of words—*run away from*. And run away seemed exactly what I had done, resulting in the guilt with which I was now contending.

There are times when I really miss my late second husband, Daniel. Solving problems is easier when you have someone to share them. He was always a good listener and sometimes had helpful advice—or at least could get closer to the crux of whatever I was mentally flailing over. When, and if, I'm wise, I try to stop and consider what he would say about whatever is bothering me, which is what I did then.

*Aha—guilt!* whispered his voice in my mind in familiar Aussie-speak. *Well, you can't cop it sweet all the time, can you, old girl?*

At sixty-three, I have married and buried two husbands— fine men both: Joe Flanagan, my high school sweetheart, an Alaskan fisherman who drowned when his boat sank in a storm, and Australian expatriate Daniel McNabb, with whom I enjoyed six fine years and who was now, not for the first time, ready to add his two cents' worth to the dilemma at hand. That was all right with me, as I still solicit and enjoy his good company on a pretty regular basis. He had a great sense of humor and the ability to take life lightly—and just then I knew he was right.

Sometimes it takes me a while to work things through for myself, but I knew that it *was* guilt tinged with remorse that I was somewhat crossly feeling, though I couldn't decide exactly what good identifying that did, or what should be done about it. No, that isn't quite right, for upon consideration I knew that I had spent a whole day and a half resisting the idea that I probably shouldn't have left Taos at all, particularly when I did—that I should stop being a coward, turn around, go back, and try to do the right thing, answer questions to which I now had possible answers.

*Your conscience is getting in your way again,* I told myself, knowing Daniel would have agreed.

But was it? Or was I obstinately getting in its way? Whichever. It was pretty obvious that I was neither satisfied nor happy with the way things had, or had not, turned out in New Mexico. Nor was I really ready to leave them the way they were, was I?

*Busybody?*

*Okay—so?*

*So you go back!*

*I do?*

There was a long semi-stubborn pause in my thinking.

With a sigh I gave in—suddenly, unexpectedly, feeling relieved.

With a decision seemingly made, I knew it would be ridiculous to set out immediately, in a storm at the end of the day. We should stay where we were for the night as planned. Then first thing in the morning, hopefully with better weather, we could head back down the road to New Mexico. With that determined I reached for a map to find a shorter route for the return trip.

I had had no specific destination in mind when I had wheeled the Winnebago out of Taos the day before in the obscuring early-morning darkness. *North,* I had told myself—with

Colorado Springs and Denver on my half-planned route. *It'll be cooler somewhere north in June than here anyway.*

Taking the closest highway out of town from the RV park where I had been for almost two weeks, I had first driven east on a winding road through the hills and valleys of the Sangre de Cristos, pulling over once to watch the road for half an hour before going on, but no one had followed. The road took me to Cimarron, where I stopped, had breakfast, and decided to spend the day, still watching the road for a black pickup truck but seeing none. It was a small, colorful community that interested me with its early Wild West connections. I like knowing things about the places I travel, and I'd learned that the ruts of hundreds of pioneer settlers' wagons passing along this last leg of the historic Santa Fe Trail were, supposedly, still to be seen. Sure enough, when I arrived, there they were.

Sleepily peaceful Cimarron, I found, had once been a luridly lawless place where the likes of Kit Carson, Annie Oakley, Buffalo Bill Cody, Jesse James—and Bob Ford, the man who killed him—Billy the Kid, Pat Garrett, and Doc Holliday were known to have stayed in its famous St. James Hotel, a short way south of town. Their presence had given rise to the establishment's violent history, demonstrated by twenty-two bullet holes that could still be seen in the tin ceiling of what had been its saloon, but which I found, upon going inside for a look, was now the dining room. Having read that the place was reputed to be haunted, I wandered around, appreciating its antique decor and original furniture, stayed for dinner, and, tempted beyond endurance, decided to abandon my motor home for one night and check in with Stretch.

Numerous guests have evidently experienced ghostly happenings of one kind or another through the years. But though

I settled comfortably in an old-fashioned bed to read *Fighting Caravans*—the novel Zane Grey penned while staying at the St. James—and waited patiently, I drifted off, so both Stretch and I spent a fine night, undisturbed by anything paranormal. Leaving the next morning, however, I did experience an oddly intense sensation of cold in the hallway opposite room number 18. When I mentioned it to the manager, I was told that room 18 was considered the most haunted in the hotel and no one was allowed inside, for it had long been occupied by an angry, malevolent presence, perhaps the gambler who in 1881 supposedly bled to death there of a gunshot wound after winning a high-stakes card game down the hall.

Back in the Winnebago—hoping that some restless spirit had not moved in during the night—I left Cimarron and headed for the Colorado border, following the route of the old trail and picking up Interstate Highway 25 a few miles before passing through Raton and leaving New Mexico. Some eighty miles later, on a whim, I turned west in Walsenburg on U.S. Route 160, telling myself that I had always wanted to see the Great Sand Dunes National Monument and might as well, being this close. But, as I drove for the next hour, I found myself briefly wondering if that was the only reason for not going directly north to Colorado Springs, where I had thought earlier that I might spend the night.

Now, as I examined the map, I saw that by taking this western side trip I had all but completed three-quarters of a rough circle and was now almost directly north of Taos, where a short two hours on another road could take me back to where I had started.

So that was that—decision validated. *And thank you, Daniel, very much,* I thought.

I fed Stretch, who woke up rested and sassy, making me wish I recovered so quickly, made myself comfort food for dinner—a toasted cheese sandwich, which I ate with a bowl of tomato soup as I listened to the wind still wailing in frustration outside.

When the galley was clean and I had double-checked the mileage of my route for the next day, I went to bed intending to continue reading Zane Grey's book about the early freighters and their wagons on the famous overland trails west. In less than a dozen pages I was nodding off over it again, so I switched off the light, curled up under my down comforter, and allowed my thoughts to return to the events in Taos that had caused such disquiet to my psyche.

"No more avoidance, Daniel," I muttered sleepily.

*Excellent! Knew you weren't a ningnong. You can nick off early in the morning. Goodnight, love.*

# THREE

As if the storm had never existed at all, the following morning dawned calm and sunny, the wind having evidently whistled off with the rain to harass someone else, leaving us a calling card in the form of a small dune-shaped pile of sand on the doorstep. By nine o'clock we were on our way, heading for Highway 160, which we would take back eleven miles to Fort Garland. There I could turn south on State Route 159, which would lead me directly into Taos before noon.

Driving with the cab windows half open allowed in the clean after-rain scent of drying sagebrush, and there were yellow flowers in the rabbitbrush along the road, which pleased me. In my own house and car, even in the dead of Alaskan winters, I always have at least one window open a bit to let in fresh air. I have never been able to understand how people can live without ever opening a window, seeming determined to run their air conditioners constantly. Being sealed into limited spaces makes me semi-claustrophobic and is part of why I dislike airplanes,

with their recycled air full of germs, and hotels with windows
that will not open so much as an inch. It feels possible that one
might breathe all the oxygen out of the air.

Stretch, an inveterate traveler, had allowed himself to be
lifted into the Winnebago and deposited in his padded basket
that hangs from the back of the passenger seat. It raises him up
for a comfortable view of the scenery, which he loves, and he
was riding, as usual, with his front feet on the edge and paying
close attention to whatever we passed. I had a thermal mug of
what was left of the breakfast coffee in the beverage holder
within easy reach and was feeling more my positive self again.
As I drove, however, I couldn't help trying to once again evalu-
ate the situation into which I was heading, by choice this time,
and recalling that I had had little choice in what I had experienced during the last few days in Taos.

Late the previous September I had left Grand Junction, Colorado, having buried my oldest and best friend, Sarah, and resolved the mystery of her premature death. It had been a sad
time for me, so I decided to do what usually raises my spirits—
travel and visit some new places.

For a couple of weeks Stretch and I toured parts of Four
Corners country, the only point in the United States where
four states—southeastern Utah, southwestern Colorado, north-
eastern Arizona, and northwestern New Mexico—meet. Those
few days of wandering canyons and deserts did as prescribed,
and I was in a better frame of mind as I headed south to
the Phoenix area, where I found a comfortable and quiet RV
park just north of the city in which to settle for the winter
months.

Winter months in Arizona, however, are not the least bit like they are in Alaska, where I have lived most of my life and am acclimated to winter weather and pleasantly cool summers. So the last week in April, when the temperature in Phoenix began to show a significant rise, I decided that any place where people felt it necessary to put cooling units in their swimming pools was soon going to be too warm for my comfort and it was time to head away from the approaching heat.

Pulling up stakes, Stretch and I took our time rambling east through Gallup, Albuquerque, and on to Santa Fe. Not a fan of large cities and traffic congestion, after a couple of days of playing tourist there, I fled happily north on the High Road to Taos, which follows the original historic trail.

Late on a sunny afternoon in early May, I rolled into town, keeping a sharp eye out for the RV park where I had a reservation. I missed it the first time through and traveled all the way from one end to the other of the main street, Paseo del Pueblo—both Sur and Norte. Halfway along, the obviously newer and wider double-lane Sur part of the street narrowed sharply and went up a small hill, creating a traffic jam where the older part of town began and continued for several blocks. Somewhere there it changed to the Norte part and, catching a glimpse of a street sign, I knew I had gone too far and paid too much attention to the casually dressed people on the street who were drifting in and out of a number of interesting-looking shops, galleries, and restaurants. Near the north end of town, spotting a BEST WESTERN sign, I pulled my thirty-foot motor home into the parking lot to ask directions, but sat for a minute appreciating the look and colors of the Kachina Lodge, a classic sort of motel built around a broad parklike area with a lawn and tall evergreen trees.

Much of the architecture of the Southwest features a traditional beautiful brown adobe. In any rainy place—Seattle, for
instance—this would quickly melt down to a large puddle of
mud. But in country with little rain the adobe not only works
well but also attractively blends into the high-desert landscape,
though I suspected that much of the modern building material
was more substantial than the original adobe bricks had been.
The motel lodge was no exception, its tan adobe accented with
wood trim painted a lovely color of medium blue that recalled
the purple-blue evening shadows of the desert country.

Leaving Stretch in the rig, I went in and found a helpful
woman at the reservation counter who marked the directions I
needed on a city map for me. Through windows in the back
wall I noticed a few people relaxing around a swimming pool.
Beyond it I could see, centered among the trees and grass of the
park area, a wide sand-filled circle with a low wall and firepit
that my helpful friend told me was used nightly from May to
October for Indian dancing.

"Come back some evening to see it," she encouraged, when
I told her I planned to stay for at least a couple of weeks. "Our
local dancers are very good and have wonderful costumes for
their traditional dances."

In a large square around the park, with plenty of parking
space, were motellike lines of individual rooms of the same
adobe and blue as the main building, with covered walkways
that provided shade for each section. The whole place was so
appealing that I almost wished I were checking in.

"I'll certainly come back for the dancing," I told her, with
thanks for the invitation. But my objective of the moment was
to get myself and Stretch settled, which meant finding a space
to park and hook up the Winnebago in the Taos Valley RV

Park, then arranging for a rental car. This is my usual practice, making it easier to get around when I spend more than a day or two in any one place in my travels. Having come the length of Taos, I could tell that, spread out as it was with both older and newer sections, a rental car would be more an essential than a luxury. Walking long distances in more heat than I am used to is not, for obvious reasons that include my senior status, my cup of tea.

On my way back along Paseo del Pueblo Norte, halfway between the Kachina Lodge and where the street narrowed, I passed a small strip mall and spotted a shop and gallery that I had on my list to visit: Weaving Southwest. Mentally marking its location, I drove two and a half miles beyond the older part of town and, following directions, easily found the Taos Valley RV Park, just a little east of the main street. I was greeted by the manager, who directed me to a space under a tree that would provide some afternoon shade for my rig.

"I thought an Alaskan might appreciate one of our cooler spaces," she told me with a smile, marking it for me on the park map that she handed me along with a receipt and a campground pass with my site number and departure date to hang on the rearview mirror. "Though it really doesn't get as warm here in the north, next to the mountains, as it does in other parts of New Mexico."

Shade on the roof of my motor home during the warmest part of the day makes a difference in how much I find it necessary to run the air conditioner. It was a rather open park, and not every space had shade trees, so I felt grateful for her consideration as I drove to locate my space under a large one. By the time I had parked, hooked up my electricity, water, and sewer connections, retrieved items that I had put away for the day's drive because they might break or rattle, and taken Stretch for a quick walk, a local dealer had showed up to deliver, for a small fee, the compact rental car, and I was ready to visit a grocery I had noted a few blocks away. On the way there I swung into the nearby Taos Visitor Center and spent a few minutes collecting some pamphlets, a detailed local map, and a phone book. After dinner that evening I settled at the dinette table with this collection and a tall glass of iced tea to acquaint myself with Taos, at least on paper. The next day would be time enough to begin the adventure in person.

It is, I found, a town, not a city, and retains, with pride and a sense of humor, its historic reputation as a more than slightly eccentric but serious art center. At 6,952 feet, nestled up against the Sangre de Cristo Mountains to the west, it boasts one of the best ski areas in the country, and I was surprised to learn that the winter temperatures and snowfall are very close to what I am used to in my rather temperate part of Alaska. It made me feel more at home than anywhere else I had been in the Southwest.

Leaning back, I looked around my motor home as I sipped my tea, still happy that I had bought it a couple of years earlier, when I decided to take off, for part of the year at least, from the cozy house in which I have spent so many years in Alaska, drive down the Alaska Highway, and see some of the rest of the world for a change. This gypsy lifestyle satisfies and pleases me, much to the chagrin of my Boston-based daughter, Carol, and her social-climbing attorney husband, Philip, on the one hand, and to the delight of my West Coast son, Joe, and his live-in girlfriend, Sharon, on the other. The Minnie Winnie provides me with the kind of leisurely travel I enjoy, allowing me to stop where and when I please. A nomadic existence almost always raises my spirits. I love to be on the road to someplace new, seeing things and meeting folks as I come to them. The company of Stretch makes it easy, for few can resist a dachshund with such an irrepressible personality.

Every time I am forced to fly I am reminded just how much I dislike it these days, especially given the security hassles and the planes packed to capacity. They don't even feed their captive audiences anymore. I suppose I should have long ago developed the trancelike forbearance and endurance of many of us Alaskans, who are almost forced to fly if we want to go anywhere else in the world. But to me, air travel is simply a torturous way to get from one place to another in the shortest possible amount of time and I try my best to sleep through it.

I may, however, have left this travel thing a bit late. For, unlike many Alaskan snowbirds, who have adapted themselves to spending the winters in warmer climes and migrating north for the warmer months, when the calendar grows thin and has only a page or two left, wherever I am I instinctively begin to think of heading north to settle comfortably into my cozy log house with a cheerful fire in the woodstove for the cold season. I like winter, with its icy, crystalline beauty and the stark contrast of snow on the spruce. In Homer, on the edge of the ocean, it seldom gets really cold, as it does in much of the rest of the state. We get our share of snow, but not the extreme temperatures of Fairbanks, for instance, to say nothing of Nome or Barrow.

But so long as it suits me and I'm able, I intend to continue exploring both the downhill side of middle age and whatever catches my fancy on the road. I felt excited and optimistic about beginning to explore Taos the next day, including Weaving Southwest, where I decided I would start.

Leaving the tourist material spread out on the table, I took care of the remains of dinner for the two of us and made an early night of it.

I had no way of knowing that the new adventure could and would be much different than I anticipated, that it would turn into one of those times when you can't seem to control much and life hands you, and those around you, lemon after lemon.

# FOUR

WITH MY BASE OF OPERATIONS ESTABLISHED AND HAVING no set schedule or commitments, I slept in a bit the next morning and got up cheerfully anticipating a day of exploration in another new and unknown place. Spreading out the detailed map I had picked up the day before from the tourism people, I studied it as I ate breakfast and found a number of places that caught my interest and sparked anticipation. On my drive through town the day before my appreciation of Taos had grown, as much for its feeling of history and attractive appearance as for the casual friendliness of the few people I had met.

Though I love my motor home, I was glad to have the compact Ford I had rented, which would make it easier to get through the narrow streets of the older part of downtown and would, I knew, make it possible to park on them later, a feat that would have been unachievable in my thirty-foot rig. So, just after ten o'clock, with Stretch in his basket—which I had transferred from the Winnebago to the passenger seat beside me—I was feeling pleased to have appropriate transportation as I pulled up in front of Weaving Southwest, my first stop of the day.

The door stood open at one side of the shop's large front window. The bright, reflected morning sun made it impossible to see through the glass, so, with Stretch on his leash, I walked in, removed my sunglasses, and stood blinking a bit as my eyes adjusted to the shade of the interior.

The long, large room was divided into three sections, front to rear, and to my surprise, having expected a clerk or two at most, I found seven or eight people. They were all busily occupied in taking down, arranging, or hanging colorful rugs and tapestries, mostly on the walls of the front section, which I could now see was set up as a display gallery. The space was full of their cheerful conversation, and no one seemed to notice me for a moment or two, as I stood watching and wondering what was going on. It made me jump when a voice spoke suddenly from just behind and below me to the right.

"Can I help you with something?"

I whirled and looked down to find a woman sitting on the floor almost at my feet; coming in half blind from the transition from bright sunlight into shade, I hadn't noticed her. In each hand she was holding a piece of finished wood, one short, the other longer, and she offered up a friendly, slightly apologetic smile to accompany her question.

"Sorry," she added, laying down the pieces of wood and standing up to hold out a now empty hand. "Didn't mean to startle you. I'm Pat Dozier, owner, manager, and general doer-of-whatever-needs-doing-next—not necessarily in that order. What seems to need doing at the moment is to put together this supposedly 'easy-to-assemble' bench. It was obviously not such a great idea to tackle this without reading the instructions, I might add."

Standing, Pat and I were about the same height. She had dark brown hair that was graying slightly at the temples, dark eyes, a quick, infectious smile—a laugh to match, I was soon to learn—and an energetic voice and way of moving. She was comfortably dressed in a denim shirt, jeans, and sandals.

"Maxie McNabb," I offered with my hand, smiling back. "And this is Stretch. I hope you don't mind my bringing him in."

Stretch, sitting at my feet and hearing his name mentioned, was looking up at her, assuming approval.

"Not at all," she assured me. "Hi, Stretch."

Sometimes I'm almost sure he smiles.

"I'm that woman from Alaska who keeps calling to order—and sometimes exchange—your yarn."

"I remember." Pat nodded. "You replaced green for blue knitting yarn to make Cheryl Oberle's ruana from the *Handpaint Country* book. Did the replacement color we sent work okay?"

"It did, beautifully, and I brought the shawl with me on this trip and wear it frequently on chilly evenings. I love the yarn colors, and I found some beads that worked well, but they aren't the same as Cheryl's."

"Oh, I wish you'd been here last week," Pat told me. "She was here—teaching a Knitaway workshop at the San Geronimo Lodge. I know she'd have loved to see how it turned out."

It was disappointing news, for I would have liked to meet Cheryl, a designer and much-in-demand instructor of knitting, whose yarns, designs, and color selections I very much admired.

"What I really need now is more of your yarn, which—besides wanting to visit Weaving Southwest—is why I came in. I'd like to make another shawl for a friend."

"Well, you've come to the source. Let's go to the back and you can see all the colors before you decide this time."

Waving an arm toward the back of the shop, she turned and we walked together past a woman behind a counter on the left, then through a center section full of books and all kinds of things weavers require in their work. I was reminded that the main focus of this shop and its people and patrons was not knitting after all, but weaving. It does seem natural, though, that people in the cold northern parts of the world knit warm clothing—especially sweaters and socks—while those in the warm south are more inclined to weave rugs and tapestries.

All my life, and especially through the cold and dark of winters in Alaska, I have worked in textile crafts—knitting, crochet, needlework, but never weaving, so I didn't recognize many of the items I saw on shelves, or in baskets, attractively, temptingly displayed. I could identify a spinning wheel when we passed one, and several varieties of large and small looms. Without stopping I could see that there were long metal needles and flat wooden ones, what looked like shuttles in an assortment of sizes, combs for tightening the weft of the wool as it was woven back and forth over a warp—a couple of terms I was sure of—and a chart that showed a whole rainbow of the colors of available dyes.

But I forgot about all of these when we reached the back of the shop with its walls of floor-to-ceiling shelves bearing hand-dyed wools in a shock of so many magnificent, rich, and glowing colors and textures that I stood speechless with the idea that I should be required to make a choice.

*Choose?* I could hardly breathe at the opulence—let alone select one over another.

"One of each?" I finally suggested to Pat, and turned to find her watching my reaction with another grin.

"You and almost everyone who comes in here for the first time," she told me. "I'll make it easier for you. Most of these are weaving yarns. The knitting ones that you'll want are over there."

She pointed to some tall corner shelves.

I could not resist going straight to the nearest and burying my hands to the wrists in the soft, springy texture of large skeins in several shades of red.

This immediate reaction drew from Pat that infectious laughter that I mentioned earlier.

"Everyone wants to touch," she told me. "You're not the first person who seemed to want to crawl right in and snuggle up."

In ten minutes I had narrowed my selections from everything in sight to a harmoniously colorful assortment with names like Log Wood, Copper, Butterscotch, Mojave Mauve, and Ragtime, with a hint of Slate Teal as an accent. The textures varied from Worsted to Jumbo Loop, Mohair Loop, Brushed Mohair, and Thick 'n Thin. Having my own pattern, needles, and beads back in the Winnebago, I was all set, and I knew my friend Carol, who had long admired my ruana, would be pleased with my decisions.

Happily satisfied, I helped carry the yarns I had chosen to the counter, where I handed Pat a credit card and she started to package up the material for the project, which I intended to start almost immediately.

"This is Mary Ann," she said, nodding toward the pleasant woman we had passed earlier, who was still at the counter. "She works here with me."

I said hello and was about to ask her if she was a weaver when my attention was attracted by a call from across the room.

"Bettye, would you hand me that piece?" asked a slender blond woman from her perch on a ladder. She had just hung up a bright red tapestry with a yellow line zigzagging through it.

"Here you go." A woman stepped over to hand up another of two, similar in size and color, which lay on the floor, evidently part of the set of three.

"Thanks. I'll help with that big one of yours when I finish these."

"Do *all* these people work here?" I asked, making my first real assessment of the work in progress. It seemed an abundance of clerks for the size of the shop.

"Oh, no." Mary Ann smiled. "There are just four of us who actually work here. Right, Pat?"

"Right. Mary Ann, Terra, Kelly, and me, of course. The others are helping to mount a show that starts day after tomorrow—Friday. They're weavers who have work in it and are here to help hang the rugs and tapestries. Come and I'll introduce you."

We made a tour of the room as I met them all, which gave me an opportunity to take a look at the weavings they were hanging, gorgeous in color and design, every one unique.

"And this is Bettye Sullivan," Pat said, pausing beside the woman who had handed up the piece to the weaver on the ladder. "She and her husband, Alex, are both weavers and dye our yarns for us as well."

Bettye was an attractive gray-haired woman with a hundred-watt smile that made you want to smile in return. Behind the glasses she was wearing, her eyes looked as blue as the shirt she had on.

"You create all those wonderful colors?" I questioned, impressed. "They're fabulous. I'd love to see how it's done."

"Well, come out to the mesa on a day when I have some to do and I'll be glad to show you," she offered. "I dye in large batches, in big hot-water tanks, but not every day. I should have a series of reds to do next week. Would you like to come then?"

"I would, very much, thanks. Shall I check here with Pat to know when and where?"

"Yes, and I'll leave you a map. I think it'll probably be—"

She stopped abruptly, interrupted by the voice of a short, round woman, who had come hurrying in the front door and seemed to be peering out from a halo of too much crinkly reddish blond hair. She was calling out urgently, "Where's Pat? Is Pat here?"

At the sound of her shrill, excited voice, everyone hesitated with what they were doing and turned to see what was happening.

The woman glanced around, spotted Pat, and trotted across to where we stood.

"Have you *heard*?" she asked. "About *Shirley*?"

"What about Shirley?" Pat asked, frowning. "Is it Shirley Morgan, you mean, Connie? She didn't come in for her lesson Wednesday, so I haven't seen her since last week."

From the frown and tone of her question, my intuition told me, she did not particularly appreciate the woman in front of her—or her demand for attention.

It seemed disruptive and offensive to have Connie thrust herself into the pleasant, creative atmosphere of the gallery—making herself significant with what was obviously a sharp bit of gossip. It was clear that she had news of some kind that she felt was momentous and that—whatever it was—to her satisfaction, it wasn't good. She took a deep breath before speaking, drawing the moment out, full of self-importance, pleased to be first with whatever she had to tell.

"Yes, that Shirley," she said. Another deep breath, then she leaned forward to almost whisper conspiratorially, "She tried to *kill herself* last night."

"*What?*"

Giving up the secretive attempt, Connie straightened and raised her voice again. "She *did*! She attempted suicide. But her neighbor in the other side of the duplex found her and called 911. She's in the hospital—probably on the *psycho* ward."

"I don't believe it," Pat told her flatly. But I noticed that her frown had now become an expression of concern that mixed with her irritation.

"Well—it's *true*. She closed the garage, got in the car, and let it run till the place filled up with carbon monoxide. If the neighbor hadn't heard the engine running and come to see, she would have died."

"When?"

"Like I said, last night—sometime pretty late, I think."

As she talked, the others in the room slowly gathered in a silent circle around us, listening closely.

"Is she going to be all right?" one of them asked.

"Who knows? All I know is that they took her to the hospital in an ambulance. The stupid people at the hospital won't tell you anything unless you're a relative."

My opinion, which I kept to myself, was that had the hospital people known just how the information that Connie had apparently tried to obtain would be circulated they would have simply hung up on her. Maybe they had. I *hoped* they had, for I could tell she was without a doubt a born scandalmonger.

Evidently Pat was thinking along the same lines.

She scowled at Connie. "I don't blame them," she said. "Who else have you told?"

"Hardly anyone. I knew you'd want to know, so I came here—practically first."

"Well, *don't*. If it's true . . ."

"Of course it's true."

"*If* it is, then spreading it around to everybody in town will just make things worse for Shirley. Can't you just keep it to— Oh, never mind. It's ridiculous to try to close the barn door when the horse is already gone."

I knew she was right about that—and that Connie had already told anyone and everyone who would listen, with no regard for the possible adverse consequences of the rumors she so insensitively conveyed. As Pat turned to me, Connie was glancing with sullen resentment at the members of the work crew, who were all going back to what they had been doing, several with disgusted looks in her direction. Having heard Pat's comment, none of them were about to ask further questions.

"Sorry," she said. "Our shop production weaver, Kelly, and I have been giving Shirley weaving lessons for the last three weeks. We had one scheduled for this afternoon, so I need to let Kelly know it's been canceled."

"I'll go and get out of your way," I told her, picking up my package of yarns. "This is all I need for now anyway. I'll come back to see you and the show this weekend."

"Oh, don't go," she said. "I thought you might like to join me for lunch. It'll only take me a minute to make the call, and then we can go. Please?"

A little hesitantly, I agreed. "If you're sure—with a show to get ready for and now this about your friend Shirley."

"I'm sure, and I'd really like it," she told me, and I could see she meant it.

I just wish now that we'd been as sure of a few things later on as she was of lunch that day.

# FIVE

I DROVE AND PAT DIRECTED US TO LUNCH AT THE APPLE Tree, a charming historic restaurant in a Victorian house on Bent Street, near downtown. I carefully chose a parking space under a huge tree so Stretch could be left in the car with a window cracked and his water bowl handy. I doubted he would be welcome in the restaurant, but he'd be fine, for it was cool there in the shade.

"I think you'll like this place," Pat told me as we walked down the street. "It's one of my favorites."

Halfway to the restaurant, the street made a dogleg to the right.

"Is the crook in it the reason it's called Bent Street?" I asked Pat.

She laughed and shook her head.

"I guess it might as well be," she said. "But I'm sure it's really named after the first governor of New Mexico, Charles Bent, who lived on it—and died on it during a Hispanic and Indian uprising in the mid eighteen hundreds. That's his house over there." She pointed to an adobe across the street. "It's a museum and gallery now."

Almost in the dogleg, the Apple Tree occupied a two-story building with boxes full of flowers under the first-floor windows. A second-story balcony shaded the front door and was painted a white that almost gleamed against the tan adobe color of the exterior.

We were greeted warmly—Pat was obviously a regular—and were escorted through to a table in one corner of a shady outdoor patio, which pleased me. One of the things I like best is being out of doors, especially when the weather is agreeable, as it was that day. Nestled as it is against the Sangre de Cristo Mountains to the north and west, Taos is cooler than communities in flatter country, southern Texas or Arizona for instance. Except for the dryness of desert country, I found its temperatures very similar to those in Homer, Alaska, where I have lived all my life. If the previous evening had been an indication, though, it would be cool enough after the sun set to make me grateful to toss a sweater around my shoulders.

Even in our Alaskan winters I take Stretch out for an everyday walk or two unless the temperature drops to an extreme or there's a blizzard howling, which happens seldom along the southwestern coast. The exercise is good for us both, and it is simply a matter of dressing for the weather. He has his own red plaid coat, and in icy weather I have been known to put booties on his feet like those worn by sled dogs.

The Apple Tree was clearly popular, for most tables on the patio were occupied. Appealing food scents and sounds filtered out of the kitchen, and the waitresses and waiters who bustled back and forth efficiently were friendly and helpful. When we had ordered lunch and been served glasses of a pleasant house wine, Pat settled back with a sigh and visibly relaxed a bit.

"I'm sorry you were subjected to Connie's tirade," she apologized. Pausing, she shrugged, then gave me a resigned half-smile. "It wasn't a very pleasant welcome to either Weaving Southwest or Taos. But I bet you know people like her, who thrive on gossip and don't know, or care, about the trouble they cause."

"I do, but it's not something I encourage. Why did Connie come to you? Is Shirley a particular friend of yours?"

"Not really. She showed up in March from somewhere in California. Not long after that she came in and said she wanted to learn to weave, so we started a class for her. We teach individuals as well as group classes—whichever is appropriate. I know she stayed in a hotel for almost a month before she found that duplex she rented, and it didn't come cheap, so I think she has money."

I really didn't want to be involved in something that wasn't my business, concerning someone I hadn't even met. But Pat seemed to want to talk about it, so I did what a friend does in that kind of situation—asked enough questions to let her know it was okay to continue.

"What do you know about her? Did she seem to have personal problems—the kind that might lead to suicide? What's she like?"

Pat considered the questions for a minute, staring thoughtfully into her wineglass before she shook her head, sighed again, and gave me an answer.

"I've been asking myself that. I wouldn't have thought so. But how do you tell? She didn't share much about herself. She did tell me that she lost her husband over a year ago. When she got here she seemed fragile about it, sort of lost without a man in her life, you know, the kind who needs one to take care of—or, more likely, one to take care of her. She seemed unused to making her own decisions sometimes. But lately, from the way she's been acting, I think maybe she's met someone—a guy I saw her with a couple of times."

The part about losing a husband caught my attention. Having lost two of my own, I remembered the shock of being suddenly alone very well and with sympathy.

When my Joe's boat sank and he drowned I was forty-four, with two young, confused, and heartbroken children who needed both parents. We had been married for just over ten years, and it had never occurred to me that we might not grow old together. He had cheerfully anticipated the two of us in rocking chairs on the porch when it came near time for our sunset. The abruptness of his absence was devastating to me, and I went into a state of denial so deep that it took my mother to shake and scold me out of it—to make me realize that I had a life to paste back together for all three of us. But it took a long time before I really accepted it.

Our lunch arrived and I enjoyed a terrific mango-chicken enchilada dish with green chiles while Pat had soup and half a Caesar salad. It was several minutes before I returned to the subject at hand with a question.

"When you said Shirley *lost* her husband, did you mean that he died?"

Pat shook her head. "No, and it might have been better for her if he had. Evidently, from the little she said, he left her for a younger woman. I *hate* that kind of thing," she said, scowling angrily. "He was some kind of executive for an investment company and pretty well off. I suspect he just wanted some young bimbo on his arm and decided Shirley was disposable. She said he married again almost immediately and the new wife was half his age."

"How old is Shirley?"

"In her fifties, I'd guess. But it's hard to tell. She bleaches her hair and tries to look younger than she is. I think she's had a face-lift—maybe more."

I thought about that, remembering when I first noticed that my laugh lines were becoming definite wrinkles and circles made their appearance under my eyes. Smoothing them out by stretching the skin with my fingers, I had stared resentfully into the mirror and contemplated the possibility of having something done surgically, as I think most women do. But it didn't take long for me to decide against it, though for some it may be a welcome, albeit temporary, solution—an escape from that tooth of time.

To me there is a certain dignity in accepting what you are, and are becoming, however age sculpts you. I can understand the impulse to look as young as possible for as long as possible, especially if your appearance is important to how you make your living, like those in the movie industry, for instance, or to the kind of entertaining required of someone like Shirley in support of her husband's professional socializing. Maybe I'm just too casual about my appearance, or too stubbornly set in my ways, but to me the value of anyone is more in the kind of person he or she is than in looks.

I looked up to see Pat regarding me with a reflective smile of understanding. "You've thought of it too, haven't you?"

"Sure," I told her, remembering that confrontation with the mirror. "Don't we all at one time or another? I decided against it for my own reasons. Then an acquaintance of mine had something go wrong with a lift that left her with an irreparable droop to one eyelid. She was devastated and it was enough to add a fear factor to the decision I had already made. I think that major efforts to defeat time are not that simple or, sometimes, wise."

"Or that inexpensive," Pat suggested with a grin and raised her wineglass. "Here's to leaving plastic surgery to the Barbie wannabes of the world and growing old the way we are—comfortable, if a bit wrinkled and fluffy."

"Agreed."

We clinked glasses and laughed together as we toasted that mutual resolution.

"Something to celebrate?" a male voice questioned from behind me.

"Hey, Ford. I expected you at the shop this morning."

Pat looked up and gave a welcoming smile to a friendly-looking man of about fifty, wearing jeans, a gray sweatshirt, and desert boots, who stepped around to the end of the table and included me with a cordial nod.

"I got a late start," he told her. "Sorry."

"Did you bring in your rug? I saved you a good space on the north wall."

"It's in the van. I just stopped in here to pick up a sandwich before heading on over to hang it."

So Ford was another weaver, I gathered.

"Join us, eat here, and I'll catch a ride back with you," Pat invited, motioning him to a seat at the table, which he took.

"Why not?" he said, turning to me and reaching across to shake my hand politely over my now cooling enchiladas. "Hi. I'm Ford Whitaker."

"Sorry." Pat apologized for her lack of manners. "This is Maxie McNabb from Alaska. Ford has a piece in the new show."

"Alaska!" he said, leaning forward with interest. "I've always wanted to go there."

*You and half the world,* I thought.

Everyone always wants to know about my home state and means to visit sometime—or already has. We talked about it for a minute or two, with me answering questions and thinking to myself that he was a charmingly natural sort with real, not polite or casual, interest. He had almost colorless gray eyes under heavy brows, thick hair as dark as my own and similarly streaked with silver, especially at the temples. It was receding into a high forehead that gave him a clean and open look. But his most attractive features to me were the creases around his mouth and eyes that affirmed a usually pleasant expression. No plastic surgery for this guy.

Interesting, isn't it, how as we grow older our faces give us away by exhibiting our most habitual attitudes for all who care to look? It made me wonder just what Shirley's face would show the world, even after the face-lift she had probably had done.

Almost immediately, as if I had offered the question aloud, her name came up as Ford turned to Pat.

"I've got some bad news about Shirley Morgan," he said seriously.

"We already know," she told him. "Typically, Connie showed

up at the shop an hour ago to give us what she considers—with great glee, I might add—the latest scandal."

He shrugged as if ridding himself of a bothersome insect crawling on his skin, frowned in distaste, and asked, "How the hell does she find out anything and everything in town that's negative or sensational? The woman's a walking *National Enquirer,* but she never gets all her facts right—just passes on the bad parts. So you know Shirley's in the hospital?"

Pat nodded.

"Did you know she's asked to see you?"

"*Me?* Why me?"

"Well, she doesn't have any family here. We have an exercise class together three times a week, but she's been skipping it lately and I've wondered why. A nurse called this morning to say Shirley was asking if I could visit, so I went over. My name and yours were the only two on her list and she wanted me to let you know she'd like to see you too."

"How long will she be there?"

"She said they'd probably let her go home tomorrow morning. I offered to pick her up, but she asked for you. Maybe she'd feel better with another woman."

Pat frowned, then nodded. "That might make sense. Did she say anything about what happened? Did she really intend to kill herself?"

Ford shook his head. "I don't know. She wouldn't talk about it. But she seemed pretty upset and confused."

"Then I'd better go as soon as we're through here," she said and turned to me. "My car's at the shop. Would you drive me?" she asked.

Of course I said I would.

Ford stayed and ate his lunch while we talked of other things and finished ours. Then Pat and I walked back to my car—where Stretch was happy to see us both—and headed for the hospital.

# Six

In the *town* of Taos nothing is really far from anything else. Holy Cross Hospital was, I found, no exception. It was quite close to the Taos Valley RV Park, where I had left my Winnebago. We were soon pulling into the parking lot of a low, modern building with hints of regional architecture in its adobe color and the long, roofed but open-sided walkway that led to the entrance.

While Pat went in to see Shirley, I put Stretch on his leash and stepped into the lobby to pick up a brochure or two before going back out to take him for a short walk in the parking lot. It never hurts to know what kind of medical assistance is available, and where, just in case you need it, especially when you're a traveling senior citizen, as I am. I don't intend to get sick or fall off the perch—as Daniel would put it—anytime soon, but you never know, do you?

Though the hospital was obviously a new facility, I learned from one brochure that it had a history that went back to 1936, when Mabel Dodge Luhan had built a house there for her son and his wife. When the young couple decided to leave Taos, she offered it to Taos to use as a hospital. Her gift was accepted and the hospital was run by a group of nuns until 1970 and thereafter by other medical services as it grew with the community and a new building was finally called for.

The name of the donor caught my attention. Mabel Dodge Luhan had been a wealthy heiress and socialite from Buffalo, familiar with many New York intellectuals and activists, who had come to Taos in 1918, where she met and married a Taos Pueblo Indian, Tony Luhan. They built a large home with numerous guest rooms, to which flocked celebrated thinkers, writers, and artists of the day, including D. H. Lawrence, Georgia O'Keeffe, Walter Lippmann, Ansel Adams, Margaret Sanger, Willa Cather, Greta Garbo, Robinson Jeffers, Thomas Wolfe, and others.

The history of a place always makes it come alive for me. So I put Mabel and Tony's house, now used as an inn and conference center, on my list of things to see during my visit and was interested to know that the hospital was linked to Mabel's historical presence in the area, though the house she had given as a hospital was, of course, long gone in favor of these modern facilities. There was, however, a picture of that original house, which I was examining when the hospital's automatically opening doors swung wide and Pat showed up again—with company.

She looked at me over the head of the occupant of the wheelchair she was pushing, rolled her eyes, and shrugged a *don't-ask-me,* letting me know that this was Shirley and that springing the woman from the hospital against doctor's orders was not her idea, or that of the frowning nurse who was trailing unhappily along behind them.

They came to a stop in front of me.

"Maxie," Pat said, "Shirley's decided she wants to go home—ah—now. I told her you wouldn't mind giving her a ride. Is that okay with you?"

With Pat nodding encouragement and the nurse shaking her head in opposition, my reaction to the request was a feeling of ambiguity and dubiousness at its wisdom. I folded the brochure with the picture of Mabel's son's house, slipped it into the pocket of my skirt, and gave Shirley a long look of assessment.

She was wearing a wraparound hospital gown—the kind that has no particular front or back and flaps flimsily open above your knees, leaving you to choose which you'd rather have exposed, front or rear. Shirley had solved the problem by tying hers in front, over another just like it that obviously opened in back.

A slight woman, thin of face and body, she looked to be the sort who has spent years automatically calculating the calories in every mouthful of food she allowed to pass her lips. Her hair was not the platinum I had mentally assumed when Pat had told me it was bleached blond, but a softer, warmer color that avoided sharp, artificial contrast, though I could see from a fraction of an inch of darker roots that her natural color was a medium brown. I could see why Pat thought she might have had a face-lift, for the skin around her eyes appeared a bit tightly smooth and there were none of the beginning signs of wrinkles that I would normally associate with the look of someone in their fifties. Without makeup, she appeared pale and tired, but who wouldn't after being almost asphyxiated and spending even a single night in a hospital?

As I hesitated, she looked up, blinking in the brightness of the midday sunlight, and gave me a quick, questioning glance that returned my assessment. Then she raised herself up out of the wheelchair and stepped close enough to offer her hand with poise and a smile. It was an attitude with which she could almost have made a hospital gown and paper slippers acceptable for a cocktail or garden party.

"I'm Shirley Morgan," she said in a polite tone of voice, "and you, Pat tells me, are Maxie McNabb."

I nodded, a little surprised at the strength of the rather lengthy pressure she was applying to my fingers. Then she swayed a little and I realized that she was not as steady on her feet as I had first assumed.

"Please," she continued pleasantly, maintaining her grip on my hand. "I realize we've never met, but I'd be grateful if you'd take me home. These *people* seem to think I'm some kind of neurotic idiot, but I *did not* try to kill myself, whatever they say. I hate hospitals and do not wish to remain in this one, so one way or another I am leaving. May I presume on your generosity, or should I call a taxi?"

"Really, Mrs. Morgan, you can't do that," the nurse said, coming around Pat to lay a hand on Shirley's shoulder. "You must come back to your room until the doctor releases you—maybe tomorrow. It's not a good idea to—"

"I can and will," Shirley interrupted her with a stubborn hint of temper, casting an entreating look at me.

Seeing Pat's encouraging expression and the suggestion of amusement that twitched her lips, I suddenly knew that, given the situation and Shirley's resolve, there was little else I could do, or wanted to.

I agreed.

# SEVEN

SHIRLEY KEPT HER ACT TOGETHER BY HOLDING ONTO Pat's arm while I retrieved my car, moved the dog's basket to the backseat, helped her in while Pat climbed in back with Stretch, and drove away from the nurse, who moved unhappily to collect the abandoned wheelchair, shaking her head in frustration as she watched us go. But as soon as we were out of her sight Shirley slumped in the seat and held her head with the heels of both hands over her eyes.

"Thank you," she said with a deep sigh. "I couldn't have stayed there another second."

"We'll have you home in just a few minutes," Pat told her, leaning on the back of the seat in front of her. "Does your head hurt?"

"It's the carbon monoxide," Shirley told her without moving. "I must have got a pretty good dose. I woke up vomiting like a sick dog, with my head splitting. It's a little better now."

"You want to talk about what happened?" Pat asked a little hesitantly.

Shirley raised her head and turned enough to give Pat a glance that was full of fatigue and, I thought, a bit of cynicism.

"There's nothing to talk about," she said. "I don't *know* what happened. I went to bed last night in my room. I woke up sometime later in a hospital bed with an oxygen mask over my face. What happened and how I got there, I have no idea. But I *did not* try to commit suicide."

As she dropped her face into her hands again I could see that there were tears streaming from her eyes.

"If I'd tried to kill myself I'd have done a better, more permanent job of it. Oh God, my head hurts so I can hardly think, but I know that much at least. If I *had* done what they assume I did, I would have made sure it worked—and maybe I should."

I looked up and saw Pat's dismay in the rearview mirror.

It was about then that I began to have real doubts that we had done the right thing in helping Shirley escape medical and psychological care.

We had left the street where the hospital was, and were traveling north on Paseo del Pueblo toward the center of town.

"Where are we going?" I asked Pat.

"Keep driving straight. I've got to go back to the shop. You can drop me off on the way and from there I'll direct you where to turn. You're in that duplex near the Fechin Inn, right, Shirley?"

As I pulled up to a traffic light, Shirley groaned.

"Yes. Well—for the time being," she confessed. "I can't stay there much longer. I don't have enough money left at the moment. He took it all. I've got to find cheaper place."

In the mirror Pat and I stared at each other, appalled at this new revelation.

*He?* Who was *he?*

I assumed at that point that she was referring to her ex-husband and that the divorce had left her with little in the way of financial support—a situation with which I was acquainted through the separations of a friend or two in the past whose exes grabbed the money, or hid it away in advance, and refused to divide it equitably, if they admitted it existed at all. Not all men are like that, of course, but men are more likely to calculate their worth and success by the amount of money they have or will make, the number and quality of things they own, and how it all compares with what other men have amassed. This seemed especially true of those leaving one wife for another, younger and prettier, waiting in the wings with expectations of the high standard of living that had attracted her in the first place. The departing husband of one acquaintance of mine simply told her, "You know how to work. Get a job," disregarding and devaluing the fact that she had worked for years in a job she hated simply to add enough to their income so that he could present an impressive social front to those in his profession who measured success by the size of their incomes and houses, the make of their expensive cars, the exclusivity and price of their club memberships.

Remember what I said earlier about lemons? Well, bear that in mind. For, without substantiation, I have to admit I presumed that Shirley's ex must be a particularly sour lemon.

There are times when you simply make choices with very little or nothing to go on. I seldom allow myself to choose on the spur of the moment and without knowing and considering what I am committing myself to, for past experience has taught me that quick decisions are usually unwise—sometimes extremely so. But it was evident that this woman was close to the breaking point and that there was more to her situation than first appeared. I was curious to know what that *more* was—and concerned that she might be serious about making suicide work. If she was, getting involved didn't much appeal to me, but from the sound of it she needed help.

It was Stretch who decided it. Loose in the back, he thrust himself far enough forward between the seats to give Shirley's elbow a sympathetic lick. Having hardly noticed he was there, she was startled by the sensation of his wet tongue on her skin and jerked around to find him staring up at her with those irresistible liquid-coffee eyes of his offering concern.

"Oh my!" she said. Then against all odds she giggled. It started with a short burst on an almost hysterical note. But as Pat, who had seen what happened, joined in tentatively, it grew more natural and relaxed. In seconds we were all laughing as Stretch, taking mirth for approval, followed his nose and scrambled into Shirley's lap, where she couldn't help petting him. Few can.

The upshot of it all was that, with Stretch's apparent approval and still wondering if it was wise, I invited Shirley to bunk with me in the Winnebago, for the night at least, and offered to help her look for a less expensive place to live the next day, whatever her reason. We dropped Pat off at Weaving Southwest, where she still had a show to prepare, then went to the nearby duplex where Shirley had been living to pick up the few things she would need until she could find a place to move into.

It was a neat frame structure with an attached garage at the end of each of its two units. An adobe wall with a gate surrounded the shallow front yard of each, and the plots were planted with cactus and other desert plants among pebbles in the space that a lawn would have occupied in less dry conditions. I was to recall later that the well-decorated and well-kept appearance of the place, inside and out, gave me my first hint that perhaps Pat had been right and Shirley had money—or *had* had money.

Being more concerned with Shirley's frame of mind, and having no idea of the price of local housing, I ignored it then. Traveling in my Winnebago, which is both transportation and living space, is practical—I don't have to make reservations far ahead for the places I visit, or follow a rigid schedule in meeting them—and economical. I can often stay in an RV park space for three or four days for what a hotel would cost for one—a condition I view as a significant luxury. I grew up in a middle-class family more concerned with well-being than wealth. We made choices as to where extra dollars would be most beneficial and enjoyable for all. While my second husband, Daniel, left me well provided for, I am careful of his investments, as he taught me, knowing that there may be more and different needs for them as I grow older.

Taking Stretch, we went into Shirley's half of the furnished duplex, which I found was larger than it appeared from the front—spacious for one person and arranged pleasantly with clean lines, cheerful southwestern colors, comfortable furniture, and an adobe pueblo-style fireplace in one corner. Beyond a table and four matching chairs, through a sliding glass door I could see a small tiled patio surrounded by another adobe wall with plantings similar to those in front, some in large pots. It was a perfect place for Stretch, so I let him out with the door open enough for him to come back inside if he liked. In the process I noticed that the door had not been locked, nor had the bar been used that fit in the track to brace it closed. I didn't think much of it at the time, just mentally filed it for consideration later.

"Would it hold you up if I took a quick shower and got dressed in something more appropriate?" Shirley asked.

I assured her it wouldn't and that she should take her time.

She disappeared into the back of the house and in a few minutes I could hear water running.

I am not generally a nosy sort, but not hesitant either if I feel it would be irresponsible to ignore the facts of anything in which I may be involved. Not completely satisfied with Shirley's declaration that she had not tried to take her own life, or that she would not try it again, I thought it might be wise to see if I could find anything to help me come to a conclusion on whether or not to depend on her word.

I didn't snoop exactly, just wandered through the place to discover whatever was there that might be enlightening.

On the table a small loom was set up, the warp half filled with wool that I recognized from Weaving Southwest. Her project for the class Pat had said she was taking, I assumed.

There was a desk in an alcove between the kitchen and the living room. I stopped beside it and found two books, one about *triumphing* over divorce, the other on being an *outrageous* older woman. Both exhibited signs of being read and reread, for they all but fell open and were full of dog-eared pages and underlining. In the first of the two I saw that in pencil Shirley had marked several sentences that referred to men's inability to understand their wives' desire for some kind of financial independence, or support for their emotional needs. As I flipped through the rest of the book, a slip of paper that had been inserted between the pages like a bookmark fell out and fluttered to the floor. It read: "Just take care of today. Take care of to-morrow when it gets here."

Evidently Shirley had been working on her problems, and in a way that seemed positive to me.

Next to the books was a laptop computer, open but turned off, a telephone, a notepad, and a coffee mug holding a collection of pencils and pens and sitting next to a dictionary, a thesaurus, a phone book, and what looked like a journal with a blue cover, all standing upright between bookends on the back of the desk. The journal tempted me, but I resisted. Somehow I have never been able to invade the privacy of someone else's personal thoughts—even those of my own children, when they were still at home.

On the wall over the desk was a small bulletin board containing a calendar and a short handwritten list of initials followed by phone numbers. Beneath four of the numbers were e-mail addresses. Listening to be sure the water still ran in the bathroom, I took a pencil from the coffee mug and quickly copied the list on a page of the notepad, stuck the page into my pocket, and replaced the items on the desk the way I'd found them.

A small, immaculately clean kitchen lay to the left of the dinette set. I stepped in and opened the refrigerator door—you can tell a lot about people by what they eat. Shirley evidently ate like a bird, a regimen I'm sure she had followed for years. The quart of milk I found on the top shelf was labeled fat free, and the other shelves held nothing but several cans of diet soda and iced tea. There was no bread or butter, no eggs, only a crisper full of vegetables and fruit and a freezer compartment empty of anything but half a dozen diet entrées.

I closed the door feeling comfortably, thankfully, and slightly—as Pat had put it—*fluffy*.

On the other side of the dinette there was a door I assumed to be a closet, and I was about to make a quick check inside it when I heard the shower turn off and Shirley leave the bathroom and go into her bedroom, so I left it alone.

By the time she reappeared, having washed traces of the hospital away and dressed in an attractive blue and white blouse and blue pantsuit that may have been denim but looked expensive enough to have come straight off Rodeo Drive, I was sitting on the living room sofa, with a recent fashion magazine on my lap, flipping pages and feeling as indisposed toward the styles they revealed as I had toward the contents of the refrigerator.

"That's better," Shirley said, setting down a small suitcase and a large green cosmetic bag that appeared to be stuffed full, with several tall containers of lotion, shampoo, and the like that, along with a hair dryer, protruded from the top. It gave me another piece of the puzzle of her attitude, for would any woman depressed enough to intend suicide actually pay attention to taking excessive care of herself? I thought not.

My own beauty regimen—if the word *beauty* can apply—consists mainly of shower and shampoo, slathering myself with moisturizer, using lots of sunblock and ChapStick, plucking my eyebrows if they threaten to get out of control, and applying a minimum amount of makeup—lipstick, eye shadow, and a touch of mascara—when necessary and if I remember. If I gave it a name, I'd be more likely to call it a maintenance routine. *Regimen* is a word that has never fit me at all well.

But, I thought, considering the probable cost, if you were going to go so far as to have a plastic surgeon *lift* anything and wanted to sustain your investment, *regimen* would probably be the exact word to use. I wondered if Shirley had a checklist.

"This is a very nice place," I told her. "How'd you find it?"

She nodded, then smiled in amusement.

"A friend recommended it, but you should have seen it when I moved in—doilies and framed embroidered mottoes everywhere. CLEANLINESS IS NEXT TO GODLINESS, for Pete's sake—pretty obvious reminder. I removed them all to a closet. The pictures are my own."

I glanced around and noticed that the three that now hung on the living room walls were attractively peaceful, with long horizontal lines typical of the southwestern landscape. Another, in the dining area, was an abstract acrylic in brilliant colors, but clean of line and uncluttered. They all looked very expensive.

"Nice choices. I particularly like the abstract," I told her.

"It was a gift," she said, "from a friend."

*Pretty significant friend,* I thought. "Was the switch okay with your landlady?"

"Well—she didn't seem particularly pleased—a little hurt even. But when I promised to put them all back before I left and showed her that I'd put them away carefully, there wasn't much she could do. I'd used the same hangers, so there weren't any new holes in the walls."

She hesitated, frowning. "I think she comes in sometimes when I'm not here," she told me. "I've found a thing or two moved from where I had put it—a book, a letter on the desk. Oh, I don't care really. It's not legal, but she's harmless, if a bit of an odd bird, and she makes great fruit-flavored iced tea."

She walked across and took the journal, the list of phone numbers, and a pen from the desk, dropping them into her bag. "Shall we go?"

Laying aside the periodical, I headed for the sliding door to collect Stretch, who came willingly. I tucked him under one arm and was locking the back door when there was a knock at the front.

Shirley went to answer it and I heard a female voice.

"Oh, Shirley. I heard the water running and hoped it was you. How are you doing, dear?"

"Fine," said Shirley, and ushered in a tall woman with graying hair, older than either of us, with a cane in one hand that she leaned on heavily in taking the first steps into the room.

"Are you sure? I didn't expect you back so soon and I would have thought that—"

Shirley interrupted.

"I'm fine—really." She turned to me. "Ann Barnes is my next-door neighbor, Maxie. Ann—Maxie McNabb—and Stretch."

So this was the snoopy landlady—the woman Connie had told us found Shirley and called for help.

Ann nodded in my direction, but her frown was all for my short-legged friend.

"Oh dear, I know I told you *no animals*. I simply *can't* rent to people who bring in animals."

"Stretch is only visiting, Ann. I'm going to stay with Maxie for a day or two and I came back to collect a few things and give you my notice. I'll be moving as soon as I find a new place."

"Oh. Well. I do think that would be best. You would probably feel more comfortable somewhere nearer a—ah—doctor, wouldn't you?"

It was evident that the woman wanted to lose Shirley as a tenant and would have told her so in a minute or two if necessary.

The bathrooms in the two units of the duplex evidently backed up to each other, so she could have either heard the shower water running or seen us arrive. She might have heard the car running in the garage next door the night before—though I wondered about that, considering that the garages were on opposite ends of the building and her speaking voice was loud enough to make me think she might be a little hard of hearing.

"Look, Ann. Whatever you may have assumed, I *did not* try to asphyxiate myself last night. But I must thank you for calling—whoever you called. It saved my life and I'm grateful."

"That's not necessary. Anyone would have called 911," Ann told her, waving a deprecating hand and returning immediately to the subject of Shirley's leaving. "So you'll let me know when you're moving? There's a week and two days left on this month's rent—nonrefundable, of course. Then there's the security deposit and the cleaning fee—and . . ."

Clearly she had carefully checked the dates before arriving, I thought grimly, but her words trailed off as my irritation overcame my reticence enough to make me step forward and interrupt. "Both of which you will return, I'm sure. This place is spotless now, or could be in ten minutes."

"Oh," she said.

She was big on *oh*.

"Well, there's always something needs doing when a tenant moves out. And considering there has been a prohibited animal on the premises . . ."

She had evidently memorized the local regulations for rentals.

"For about half an hour and not inside—out on the patio," I told her, tightening my hold on Stretch, who was wriggling to get down.

"Still . . ."

"I think you'll find it legally advisable to refund it all except what's left of Shirley's rent for this month—if she moves before it runs out. Ready, Shirley?"

With a twinkle of relief and amusement in her eye, she nodded, picked up her suitcase and cosmetic bag, and followed me past her landlady to the front door.

"Thank you again, Ann," she said sweetly as we went by. "You'll make sure the front door is locked, won't you—*dear*?"

I was glad my back was turned. There's no use adding insult to injury with a chortle—even if deserved—when the woman still holds your money.

It was encouraging to know that Shirley still had spunk.

# EIGHT

MUCH LATER THE SUN WAS SETTING IN STRONG, MARVELOUS colors—amber, scarlet, and deep purple blues in contrast to the gilded edges of a few billowy clouds—brighter than what we see in Alaska, though we often have spectacular colors, especially during the summer months, and reflected from the many waters of our state they can be impressive.

For half an hour Stretch and I had been making our way back to the RV park, having walked a long way toward the eastern mountains. Estes Road had risen just enough as we strolled to allow me to see across Taos to part of the western mesas that were now out of sight as we turned in at the park gate and headed toward the Winnebago, where I had left Shirley asleep, as she had been for hours.

The park sites were surrounded with vegetation natural to the area—rabbitbrush and sagebrush, which I could smell as I stopped to examine a prickly pear cactus next to the concrete slab of an empty parking space. A magpie was picking at something in the gravel of the drive near the office. I could hear the voices of smaller birds in the trees and brush—twitters and chirps from sparrows, finches, the *dee-dee-dee* that names the chickadee—and a sudden flash of yellow gave me a quick glimpse of a grosbeak, though I could not identify its call among the conversation of other birds. I had seen ravens elsewhere in town, but was on the lookout for a bluebird, which is not common to Alaska.

The cottonwoods were shedding the pale, creamy fluff that gives them their name. At the smallest suggestion of a breeze it rolled into small spheres that collected together in waves of white and wafted across any open space to pile up against whatever stood in the way of their passing. I picked up a handful and found it soft as the down in my favorite comforter.

Stretch sniffed at another pile. Then, as the feathery stuff clung to the dampness of his nostrils, he sneezed and blew half the pile of fluff away.

"Nice try, but it's not edible, you silly galah," I told him—*galah,* an Aussie word I had picked up from Daniel, referred to someone easily duped. Stretch had been his dog when we met—just a puppy then, now middle-aged in dog years.

"Come along. I have a drink and some dinner in mind."

It appeared to be a slow time of year at the RV park—only three or four other spaces were filled. We walked through to reach ours, which was close to the back. Halfway along the access road and nearest to where I had parked the Winnebago I passed a couple relaxing in the evening shade of their forty-five-foot Class A Fleetwood American Heritage. It was huge and flat-fronted like a bus, and the four slide-outs that extended, two on each side, looked as if they would expand the interior space into what was in effect an apartment, or a small house on wheels. I couldn't imagine wanting to drive a rig that

big—knew I could, but wouldn't want to. But I reminded myself that some people give up a land-based existence, sell their
houses, and buy motor homes large enough to live in year-
round. Often they find a park in an area they like and stay
there for months at a time. I, on the other hand, have my house
in Alaska to drive or fly home to, and usually do for at least part
of the summer months. Otherwise, I am happy and comfortable in the thirty-foot Class C Minnie Winnie, which is just
the right size for Stretch and me. Everyone to his own tastes
and needs. The couple spoke, and I smiled and nodded as we
passed.

The sun disappeared, leaving only a hint of departing pink
on the underside of a cloud or two. It was that twilight time of
day that the French call *l'heure bleu,* when artificial lights appear brighter than they really are and the air itself seems to
hold a pale lavender-indigo hue. The sweet scent of some
blooming flower floated in, but I couldn't identify it.

I could hear the sound of classical music on the radio when
I arrived at my rig and opened the door to find Shirley sitting at
the dinette table, with a half-emptied glass of iced tea in front
of her.

"There you are!" she welcomed me with the first real smile I
had seen on her face.

The sleep had apparently done her good.

"Here we are," I agreed. "Feeling better?"

"Oh yes—*much,* thanks. And I *love* this place," she told
me, enthusiastically waving one hand to indicate the whole interior of the Winnebago. "I've never been inside one before
and it's fascinating, so I took a look around. I hope you don't
mind. Everything fits together like a puzzle and is so conve-
nient and livable. The kitchen is terrific, and the way the sofa

slides out—and the bed. How do they do that? And how does all the plumbing, water, and electricity work? What happens if you can't find a place like this and have to spend the night in a supermarket parking lot? I've seen these things parked at Wal-Mart, but they don't have connections to power, do they?"

As her questions piled up faster than I could answer, I thought what a different person this was from the almost haggard woman who had practically fallen onto my bed as directed, been tucked in under a light throw, and gone to sleep almost as soon as her head hit the pillow.

Stretch, beggar that he is, trotted over to her, tail wagging furiously, and allowed himself his due in pets and pats.

A dog is not a bad buffer zone in allowing strangers to get to know each other more easily.

"I'll feed this mongrel, then make us some dinner," I suggested. "I'm thinking chops and salad. Is there anything you can't eat?"

"No, but let me help."

"There's really just room for one in the galley—its only drawback," I told her. "What you *can* do is pour me a shot of the Jameson you'll find in the fridge, along with a glass of ice water. And help yourself to whatever you want while you're at it."

"I'm fine with iced tea," she said. "I probably don't need alcohol after last night's trauma."

Reminded of the events of the preceding night, I knew there was a lot I had wanted to ask her, but earlier it had been evident that what she needed was rest, physical and mental, and all the questions would wait. Even now, as I assessed a return of at least part of her energy and enthusiasm, they needn't be thrown at her all at once, but could be taken one or two at a time, as she was willing to consider and answer them. They could wait again, at least until after we had eaten. Then I would see. So I answered her questions about the Winnebago and, as I cooked, we talked about the places I had visited since obtaining my motor home.

Shirley herself brought up the subject of her trip to the hospital when we had finished dinner, cleaned up the galley, and put away the dishes—I washed, she dried and put away—and were once again sitting at the table with mugs of Constant Comment.

"You know," she said, setting down her tea, "I'm still trying to figure out what happened last night. How the hell did I get from my bed to the car in the garage anyway? That's where Ann told them she found me. But I don't remember any of it and none of what they said makes any sense."

I said nothing for a minute, giving her room to continue if she liked, but she just shook her head in apparent confusion and discomfort.

"What *do* you remember?" I asked simply.

"Just what I said this afternoon. I was very tired and worried—about my finances. I remember going to bed at just after ten o'clock. Later I woke up once from a bad dream but went right back to sleep. Then—nothing. I woke up in the hospital sometime very early this morning, having no idea where I was, or how I got there. Is it amnesia? Can I possibly have blanked it out? I don't think so. I know I don't sleepwalk and that I had no intention of suicide. There's got to be more to it than that—but what?"

More to it, indeed. I couldn't help agreeing.

As we stared across the table at each other, I suddenly knew that whatever had happened to her, my feelings about Shirley had changed. I didn't know exactly why, but I had decided that she believed what she was telling me—that she really didn't know what had happened to her.

Was there any way to find out?

# NINE

I HESITATED, NOT WANTING TO FORCE HER TO TALK BUT
wanting to know more about her and her situation, especially
that comment she had made in the car about someone—*"he"*—
taking all her money. It seemed a reasonable place to start.

"If you don't mind my asking, why do you think your ex-
husband took your money?" I questioned.

She looked up, startled at the subject switch and at my as-
sumption. "Oh *no!*" she protested sharply. "It wasn't Ken I was
referring to. Our divorce was pretty equitable and fair. Most of
my share is invested in solid stocks and bonds, and the interest
gives me regular payments for living expenses—rather gener-
ous, really. What I did was to stupidly pull a hundred thousand dollars from my savings and make what I thought was a
short-term loan to help out a friend. It has now disappeared,
along with the guy, leaving me temporarily with a cash flow
problem."

It was not at all what I had expected to hear. I reminded
myself again that making assumptions is never a good idea and

wondered why I had been so willing to do so when I knew that neither of the men I had been married to would ever have tried to cheat me out of what we had shared between us in assets. Life with fisherman Joe had been a bit financially precarious at times—we were like almost everyone getting started and raising children when your bankroll depends on and fluctuates with the size of an annual catch. But Daniel, even before we married, had invested wisely and had left me well taken care of, bless him. Without exception he had never presumed me incapable of dealing with finances and trusted me to administer our investments when he was gone, with advice from a dependable counselor as needed.

Divorces can get ugly, of course. People, even good people, go a little crazy, and money is a way of hitting back at what hurts them. Still, I should not have assumed the worst of someone I knew nothing about.

"So-o." I spoke slowly, thinking fast in new directions. "You're not destitute, just temporarily short? Wouldn't Ken help out?"

"Oh, I *couldn't* ask," she said, her expression turning to distress similar to what I had seen from her in the car as we left the hospital. "It's so embarrassing that I let myself get into this situation—that I was so easily taken in. I couldn't have him know I was dumb enough to hand that much money to someone I didn't know well without some kind of formal guarantee that it would be returned. I just couldn't . . ."

The sentence trailed off. She turned toward the window, staring out into the dark, and I could see the frustration on her face.

"I feel like such a fool, Maxie. It's degrading and I'm ashamed that I was so emotionally needy."

I was beginning to have more than a glimmer of an idea of what must have happened. Somehow, someone had scammed her, and well.

"Taken in by who, Shirley? You said this afternoon that *he* took all your money. I'm sorry I took it for granted it was your ex-husband. Who did you mean? If you want to talk about it to someone, I'm a stranger, which may make it easier."

She turned back to me and there was something besides frustration in her eyes—a deep and thoughtful anger.

"He said his name was Anthony Cole," she said. "But I imagine that was a lie—like everything else he told me, damn him!"

*Anger's healthy,* I thought, and nodded to encourage her.

"Who is this man? How and where did you meet him?"

"At the Adobe Bar in the Taos Inn downtown. One night almost two months ago I went with two other weavers from Pat's shop to hear a flamenco guitarist. It's a popular place that's always crowded, and this is a pretty small town so most people seem to know each other. We sat with a few others and one of the women introduced me to Tony, so I assumed he was part of the local group. He was attractive and easy to talk to. You know—he paid attention to me and I was flattered. It's been a long time since any man paid that kind of attention. Somehow women of my age are sort of invisible to men, and I had missed the attention—a lot. The divorce may have been equitable, but my ego took an enormous beating. When he offered to drive me home I wound up staying on after the others left. That's how it started."

It seemed a pretty ordinary start, though I understood what she meant about being invisible, having noticed or experienced the attitude myself a time or two. I remembered one evening after Joe was killed and before I met Daniel, when I was sitting in a bar in Homer talking to a friend of about my age who from his attentiveness I had assumed was interested in me. I was enjoying our comfortable, lively conversation when the door opened and in sashayed a tall, long-legged blonde in her mid-thirties, dressed in a short skirt and a tight knit top, clearly chosen to accentuate her obvious physical attributes.

My friend somewhat absently finished his sentence to me as his eyes followed the younger woman all the way across the room to where she paused hipshot beside a distant table. Then he sighed, turned back to me, and asked a little wistfully, "Do you think I'm too old for her?"

It took a few seconds, but for once in my life I came up with the precisely right and appropriately timed answer—*"I certainly hope not!"*—and terminated the conversation.

At the memory I once again gave myself a mental high five as I nodded encouragement to Shirley, which was all it took for the whole story to come tumbling out, along with her hurt feelings, embarrassment, and more of that spark of anger I had recognized earlier—slowly growing icy in tone. As she talked I could tell she was watching closely for my reaction, which I took for discomfiture at her own humiliation, so I was careful to maintain a sympathetic, nonjudgmental expression.

To Shirley, Tony had seemed the perfect escort for an older woman newly divorced and unaccustomed to dating—nonthreatening, undemanding, considerate, and respectful. He had done everything right—took her to dinner, brought her flowers and small gifts, listened with interest and understanding to the tale of her divorce, cuddled and comforted. Within a week they had been intimate, in two he had all but moved in, even charming the landlady, Ann Barnes, out of any reservation or disapproval at his presence next door. In fact, Shirley told me, Ann had practically simpered at his attention, though in private he had expressed condescension for her gullibility.

"Why couldn't I see that he was playing the same game with me?" she asked. "How could I have fallen for it? I was just so damn hungry for validation and approval."

Tony had spun another appealing lie about himself, painting a picture designed to put her at ease with his circumstances. He was, he said, a senior vice president of a large Chicago-based contracting business that designed and built facilities for a variety of industrial corporations—manufacturing plants, warehouses, airports, and shipping plants. As an example, he had told her that his company had built an international routing facility for FedEx in some southern state she couldn't remember.

"What was he doing in Taos?" I asked her, for it seemed an odd place to find someone like the person she had described.

"He said it was a sort of working vacation—that he went back and forth to Santa Fe, where he was engaged in a series of meetings to finalize a new project. And he *was* gone, several times overnight, once for two days. He called me from there— or at least he said that's where he was. I had no reason to think otherwise."

When he came back from these trips, besides the usual flowers, he brought her other thoughtful—or, I thought, perhaps carefully calculated to seem thoughtful—presents: books on weaving, a musical jewelry box, lingerie, along with cards to make her laugh or feel cared for.

"He even gave me an antique ring that he said was a diamond that had belonged to his mother. I'm good with jewelry, so I knew right off that it wasn't real—that it was a cubic zirconium. But I didn't want to hurt his feelings, so I didn't say anything. That vanished along with Tony. And along with several valuable pieces of my own jewelry, I might add. So I guess he could tell the difference all right."

Shirley frowned and took a sip of her tea before continuing.

He had, she said, come back from his last trip to Santa Fe in a distressed mood. The negotiations on the new project had hit a snag, he told her. To top it off, he had become aware of a piece of property that was perfect for what they wanted to build, but he couldn't get the earnest money fast enough, before it was picked off by another interested buyer, so he was about to lose it.

"He said that corporate wheels ground slowly in the head office, that they were in the process of another purchase and it would be a week before anything could be done. In three days the property would be gone for lack of nothing but the basic earnest money and he would be blamed when the whole project self-destructed. I thought he was really upset.

"When I found out it was a hundred thousand I was uneasy, but I knew that I had it, or could have it in hours. I trusted him, Maxie. He had been so good to me and I knew it would only be a week before I had it back. He played me just right, didn't he? Like a fool, I had my California bank arrange the transaction with a Taos branch and gave him a check a day and a half later. He left for Santa Fe the next morning and that was the last I saw of him—and my hundred thousand. The check was cashed immediately, and that was two weeks ago. What the hell could I have been thinking? The *bastard!*"

She buried her face in her hands and burst into tears again.

I sat staring across the table at her and thought about how we sometimes fool ourselves—justify the errors we make—often with purpose. This was an intelligent woman who should have known better, who actually *did* know better. She had simply ignored what she knew for what she wanted to believe. But there are all kinds of reasons why we don't follow our best judgment when we should. Then, sometimes, when we are forced to face the reality of our mistakes, we have to do the best we can with whatever we have left.

I handed Shirley a box of tissues and made her another cup of tea.

When the tears stopped she sat back, giving me a tentative look or two to see if I was appalled at her folly or had believed her. I couldn't really tell which. I leaned forward on my elbows, cup between my hands, and asked mildly, "What are you going to do about it?"

"Do? What *can* I do? I can't even think right this minute, but I haven't been able to come up with anything to do."

"Well," I said, "let's leave it till tomorrow and see if together we can work something out, okay?"

She nodded and the conversation ended. I wondered why she hadn't gone to the police, but decided I would wait until tomorrow to ask her. What she had told me was enough for the night. We were both tired and disinclined to take it any further.

From somewhere far away in the direction of the mountains the drawn-out wail of a coyote came floating in through an open window. Stretch sat up from where he had been dozing on the floor at my feet, suddenly all attention.

"Don't even think about it," I told him. Then, with one of Daniel's verbal Aussie twists: "You wouldn't have an earthly in a dustup with that one."

Shirley stared at me, curious at the shape of my comment, so I explained about Daniel, my absorption of his Aussie slang, and why it was appropriate since Stretch had been his dog when I met him.

She listened and smiled a little, then yawned a huge yawn, covered politely with her hand, and I suggested it was time to call it a night.

She, like most non-RVers, was intrigued when I took our mugs from the table and began the process of converting the dinette into a bed. It's easy enough. I store extra sheets, blankets, and pillows under the benches, so I raised the lids to remove them, swung the table down on its wall support to rest on the cleats attached to the front of each bench, and arranged the cushions we had been sitting and leaning back on to cover the bed area.

"That's ingenious. I think I could live in one of these motor homes," Shirley said with a sigh that sounded a little envious, as she helped me put linens on the bed. "It's just the right size, isn't it? It must be fun and satisfying to be able to travel like you do from place to place and still be at home."

"It suits me well enough," I agreed.

We turned in for the night—Shirley in her dinette bed, Stretch and I in our usual ones in the back.

In a few minutes I could hear the small sound of her snoring lightly and knew that waiting until the next day for any further discussion had been a good idea. What she had allowed to happen was irresponsible in the extreme. But, as my grandmother used to say to my mother about my mistakes, *The girl needs building up, not tearing down.*

Going to sleep was not so easy for me as for Shirley. There was something bothersome in the back of my mind that I couldn't seem to get hold of—something that I needed to recognize about her story. But I couldn't dredge it up, and the harder you try with something like that, the farther away it slips. It might be something that would answer itself in further conversation the next day anyway. Finally I gave up and let it go, hoping it would come clear in the morning, and went to sleep.

I did not rest well, however. With someone I did not really know sharing my space, even someone I had purposely invited, I was subconsciously aware of every time she moved or rolled over in bed, and I woke more than once in the dark to think awhile before I went back to sleep.

Stretch was restless as well, but his wakefulness had more to do with what he heard outside, as the coyote howled again later and another answered from farther away, toward the mountains. It was a long, lonely sound that reminded me of the wolves that we have in the wilds of Alaska and seldom see.

There are predators of one kind or another almost everywhere, even the human kind. The man that Shirley had described was certainly a human wolf, I thought, and then changed my mind. He was more like a coyote, I suspected—without the confidence of a wolf but ready to slink in and snatch whatever appealed to him from whoever it belonged to, wherever it could be embezzled, with no sense of shame, just following the path of least resistance in assuring his survival at the expense of someone else.

Hearing Stretch turn around in his basket next to my bed and settle down again, I turned over and soon drifted off myself.

# TEN

IT WAS AFTER SEVEN WHEN I WOKE, FEELING TIRED, BUT able to sleep no more. For a few minutes I lay there, staring at the motor home ceiling with its vent open an inch or two to let in fresh air.

When I rolled over to look down, Stretch was already out of his basket, sitting by my bed and looking soulfully up at me, so I knew he needed to go out. A quick peek told me Shirley was still asleep, so I put on a robe and slippers, and—taking my shower bag, towel, and fresh clothing—went quietly out the door and headed for the campground shower rather than using my own.

Stretch, after pausing to piddle next to a handy shrub, scampered after me and caught up as I passed the large Fleetwood, where no one seemed awake yet.

Clean and more alert after my shower, my next thought was to satisfy my immediate craving for coffee, as strong as possible, with milk and sugar. I can't tolerate artificial sweeteners. For me, as for others I know, they leave an unpleasant aftertaste. I am active and stubborn enough not to worry about my weight, and though I guess every woman thinks she could stand to lose a few pounds, I stick with real sugar.

A quick look assured me that Shirley was still asleep, so I took along breakfast for Stretch and drove out Estes Road to Paseo del Pueblo, where not far up the street I found a small but pleasant-looking restaurant open for business. While breakfast for a dachshund was served in the car, I walked in to find the place surprisingly roomy and filled with the appealing scent of fresh coffee and good things frying on the grill.

Awaiting the eggs, bacon, and toast I had ordered to go with the coffee that had been brought along with the menu by a friendly waitress with a fresh flower in her hair, I watched a steady stream of customers come in, many for food to take away with them, and assumed that most were on their way to work. While they waited for their order, a couple of young men in paint-stained overalls and battered work boots flirted with the cashier in a cheerful way that told me they were probably regulars. She gave as good as she got in the verbal exchanges and waved them off with a "See you tomorrow."

I sat for most of an hour, enjoying my breakfast and a subsequent coffee refill, watching the human traffic, and I took two large Styrofoam cups of it with me when I finally decided it was time to be gone—one for Shirley, who I thought would probably be up by the time I returned.

Stretch had cleaned his bowl and was watching for me through the back window. Ready for travel when he heard the click of the lock, he came scrambling forward into the passenger seat. I got in and secured the coffee cups in the double beverage holder.

"Yes, I'm finally back."

I gave him a rub for his ears and a pat for his back before I started the car. He rolled over and presented his stomach for attention as well, so I scratched it for him and he licked my hand in thanks.

"You're a bonzer boy, you are," I told him, amused.

Pulling back into the campground I parked next to the Winnebago and noticed that the shades were raised, though I didn't see Shirley through the window over the dinette. The door was unlocked and, not wanting to startle her, I called her name as I stepped in, waited for Stretch to make it up the steps before closing it again, and set the two cups of coffee on the counter by the galley sink.

There was no answer. The dinette had been returned to its configuration as table and benches, and the linens put away under a bench along with the pillows. The galley was as clean as we had left it. She had not made coffee or breakfast for herself.

The doors to the bath and bedroom stood open and both were empty. One of the towels I had put out for Shirley was damp and there was a hint of toothpaste on the sink drain, so she had used the bathroom. When I noticed that the green cosmetic bag she had left there the night before was nowhere in sight, I stepped back to the front of the coach and found her suitcase missing as well.

I had been away for just over an hour. In that time and for some reason of her own, Shirley had gone, taking everything that belonged to her and leaving practically no trace in my living space that she had spent the night.

Making another search of the whole interior, I found that she had left no message to give me answers—or even to thank me for the hospitality. It seemed improbable and odd, considering her polite behavior of the previous afternoon.

I automatically added my own sugar and milk to one of the cups of coffee and sank onto a bench at the table, feeling dumbfounded and confused. What could have made her just take off like that?

As I sipped absentmindedly at the coffee, motion outside the window opposite the dinette caught my attention and I looked out to see that the man I had noticed the night before was disconnecting the hookups to his Fleetwood in preparation for the road. Maybe he had seen Shirley go, I thought, getting up, out, and across to his space, leaving Stretch inside.

"Yes," he told me, straightening at my question. Wearing rubber gloves, he had been releasing a sewer connection, so he didn't offer to shake hands, for which I was grateful. "She came and asked if we would call a taxi for her. We did, it showed up, and she left in it about—oh, maybe a half hour ago. No, she didn't say where she was going and didn't leave any message with us. Sorry."

"And she was alone?"

"Yes."

I thanked him, went back to my space, and climbed in to sit again at the table, thinking hard.

What could have motivated her to take off so abruptly? I remembered my hesitation at inviting her the day before and told myself that perhaps I should have paid more attention to my instincts and responses to other people's troubles. Looking back, I recalled that before going to sleep I had had a feeling that there was something bothersome about her story that I couldn't identify. But it was no clearer for sleeping on it than it had been then.

I reviewed what Shirley had told me the evening before about what had happened to her and suddenly remembered her saying that the man who had taken her money had also taken several pieces of her jewelry. As I also remembered the way I felt she had watched me to see if I believed what she was telling me, the thought raised my hackles. With sudden misgiving, I stood up, went back to my bedroom, and opened the drawer where I keep the few pieces of costume jewelry I travel with, photographs I have taken or been given, extra sunglasses, an address book—the odds and ends that don't ever seem to have a specific place they should be kept, so you collect them all together.

Everything was there. Nothing had been touched.

Next I checked the daypack in which my cameras reside on the floor of the closet. They, too, were where I had left them, with the tripod and extra film. My laptop computer was where it belonged, on a high shelf of the same closet. It is insured, as are the cameras, but I would have hated to find them missing.

I do not travel with anything of real value or that I would be devastated to lose. That is what safes and safe-deposit boxes are for. I carry around only what I need and will use. Anything else I either forgo, get rid of, or send home.

When I bought the Winnebago and knew I would be a lone traveler, except for Stretch—who is not the same threat a German shepherd would be but is great company—I hired a trusted neighbor who was good at woodworking to build me a secret compartment that would be extremely hard to find if you didn't know it was there. In it I keep a shotgun, extra shells, and any small amount of cash I don't want to carry around. Anything else of importance, or that might be a temptation to a thief—identification, medical information, cell phone, credit cards, and keys—goes where I go, in the bag in which I carry my wallet.

So Shirley, money problems or not, had taken nothing but what belonged to her. I felt a little embarrassed at my qualms, but you never know, do you? I might have been letting my imagination run away with me, but then again I might not. I still felt there was something unsettling about the story she had told.

It was possible—even probable—that she had been embarrassed at telling even a stranger the details of what she viewed as a huge personal weakness of misjudgment—at revealing so much of herself. That made quite good sense. Everyone has felt that way at one time or another. If that was the case, Shirley, humiliated, discomfited, and reluctant to face me, might well have left instead. Recalling verbal lapses of my own, something Dorothy Parker wrote about wishing she had not talked so much at a party floated into my head. The night before hadn't been a party, but the idea was close to the same in wishing one had kept one's mouth shut.

Shirley also had finding another place to live on her mental list of things to do.

But it really didn't matter why she had gone, did it? In any case, I wasn't about to go chasing after her to find out where and why. She had probably gone back to the duplex, where she could live at least until the rent ran out. Yes, it would have been polite to tell me she was leaving, but did I really care? I decided I didn't. In fact I was a little relieved to be rid of her problems, wasn't I? I decided I was.

I considered calling Pat to let her know that Shirley had disappeared, but decided it would be sufficient to mention it when I saw her again in person, since it was clear Shirley had chosen to leave on her own.

The coffee had gone tepid, but I didn't mind. I'll happily drink it at whatever temperature it happens to be. If it gets too cold I sometimes add ice. Sipping at it, I looked out the window, saw that it promised to be a warm, sunny day, then switched gears and decided that maybe it would be a pleasant time to explore some of downtown Taos. On my way to lunch with Pat the day before I had noticed Moby Dickens, a bookstore where I could probably find some information on the history and people of the area.

Leaving the restaurant that morning, I had seen copies of the weekly *Taos News,* which had evidently just come out, for the vending machine was close to full, so I bought one, planning to take a look at the ads before making another visit to the grocery. I pulled it across the table, where I had dropped it on the way in, and, folded inside, found a flyer for Raley's, the supermarket I had previously visited. In a few minutes I had made a list from it of things I needed, knowing there would undoubtedly be a few other items in the basket when I made it to the checkout counter. After spending part of the day exploring, I would stop at the grocery on the way home.

Laying the flyer aside, I glanced at the front page and was startled by a headline just above the fold: MURDER VICTIM FOUND IN DYER'S VAT. Remembering Bettye Sullivan, the woman I had met at Weaving Southwest, I unfolded the paper, scanned the article, and was relieved to find that the incident had not involved the vat in which she dyed yarn for the shop, but another that was used by a local weaver to dye yarn for her own projects. Going back, I read it through.

Two days earlier, the weaver—a woman named Doris Matthews—had built a fire under an outdoor fifty-gallon vat in preparation for dyeing a large amount of wool for a rug she intended to start, but she noticed an unusual smell and an objectionable residue floating on the surface of the water as it began to simmer. Though the vat had been covered, she thought that perhaps some bird or animal had found its way in and drowned, so she put out the fire and checked to see. She discovered not an animal but a human body and called the police.

In the process of retrieval it had become apparent that the victim was a man, but the condition of the body made him, for the time being, impossible to identify, to tell how long he had been there, or to determine if death had occurred before or after his immersion in the vat.

The story concluded with an appeal by the police for any possible information concerning the identity of the victim, referring readers to Taos Crime Stoppers.

I put down the paper and thoughtfully took another swallow of my coffee. What a horrific thing to happen. I could imagine the woman's shock at finding a body in her vat and wondered how long it had been there before she'd decided to dye her wool and how long after she had built the fire that began the cooking process. My stomach turned over and I realized that I had pulled my lips away from my teeth in a grimace of revulsion. It was a chilling and repulsive thought, but one that would go through the mind of anyone reading the article. The police would be wondering the same things, but I imagined that it would be possible for forensics specialists to figure it out.

It seemed like the past two days had somehow been tangled up one way or another with weavers. Could this Doris Matthews be someone Pat would know? I thought it probable that most weavers in the area would at least know of each other, and there seemed to be a lot of them, which made sense in a town famous for its arts and crafts.

That weavers would collect in New Mexico also made sense, as the Southwest is well known for its weaving and many of

them must do their own dyeing. I had read that the tradition
and patterns had sprung mainly from the Pueblo and Navajo
peoples, who had woven fabric even before the first Spanish
colonists and their weavers arrived in the late 1500s with herds
of churro sheep, the wool of which had a large and continuing
impact on the craft because of its long, light fibers and ten-
dency to take dye well. The Navajo, for instance, who had used
only nonanimal fibers in their weaving, soon switched almost
totally to wool.

Thinking of Pat, I decided to make another stop at Weaving Southwest to see if Shirley might possibly have contacted
her after leaving me. I also wondered what she would have to
say about the incident in the news, which she undoubtedly
would be aware of by now.

"Come along, Stretch. Let's go," I told him, knowing the
word *go* would start his wheels turning, which it did. By the
time I collected myself, he was waiting for me by the door.

# ELEVEN

THE SHOP, WHEN STRETCH AND I REACHED IT, WAS VERY quiet and for a moment or two I thought no one was there, though the front door had been open. Then Mary Ann stepped out from behind the wall that divided the front from the center section, where she had been reordering items on shelves.

"Hello," she called. "I bet you're here to pick up the yarn you forgot yesterday. I'll get it for you."

With Connie's gossip and Shirley as a distraction, in the preceding hours I hadn't even remembered the yarn I had selected so carefully. Sometimes I think I'm not just having senior moments, but losing my mind. One of these days, if I'm not careful, I'm going to forget where I've parked the Winnebago, especially since I periodically move it from one place to another in my travels.

I thanked her and took the package, intending not to lay it down until I reached the car, but that didn't last long.

In answer to my question about Pat, Mary Ann told me she was on her way and would be there shortly, so I decided to wait.

Mary Ann went back to her work and, setting the package of yarn back on the counter in plain sight, I wandered over to take a look at the bookshelf, where I found two that interested me. One, *The Thread of New Mexico,* was a catalog of an exhibition of the same name that had taken place at the Albuquerque Museum several years earlier and that had featured "weavings by contemporary weavers of the three dominant cultures in the region." It was full of color pictures of wonderful tapestries and rugs, traditional and otherwise. The other, *The Weaving, Spinning, and Dyeing Book,* by Rachel Brown, was, Mary Ann told me, the *bible* of everything to do with weaving, from types of looms to the techniques used on them. It explained weaving very clearly and thoroughly, making me feel I had missed out on a significant textile craft. Why not buy a small table loom, I thought, and try it?

Was there one that would be suitable for a traveler to use in a motor home? I asked Mary Ann.

With her help and advice, I chose what was called a school loom, about fifteen inches wide and two feet tall, which folded flat when not in use and could be stored in my closet. From that we began to collect everything else I would need to start a simple first piece: strong neutral thread with which to warp the loom, a selection of wonderful colors and textures of weft yarn, several long metal needles for weaving yarn between the alternate warp threads, a batten to pack the yarn together tightly, and a wooden comb with a handle and many teeth for the same purpose over a smaller area. Noticing a basket full of attractive flat wooden needles, I picked up one of those as well, partly just because I liked the shape and feel of the smooth, finished wood in my hand.

Mary Ann was adding another sizable purchase to my credit card and putting both the items for weaving and yesterday's forgotten yarn together in plastic bags when Pat came hurrying in, her own coffee in hand, stopped to take a look, and laughed.

"Couldn't resist, right? This place has a habit of inspiring that sort of thing," she told me. "Be careful—weaving's addictive, and you soon may find you've given up knitting for it. If you want help getting started, I can give you a few individual sessions, like the ones Kelly's been giving Shirley."

I hadn't thought of that, but it seemed like a good idea, so we agreed on the following Monday, after the weekend opening of the new show.

"You will come for the reception, won't you?" Pat asked. "It starts at seven tomorrow night."

I realized I had forgotten that the next day would be Friday, though the newspaper should have told me, but I assured her I wouldn't miss it. Not having a job to go to, children to send to school, community activities and social commitments, or other date-sensitive demands on my time, I sometimes let days slip by without paying much attention to the day of the week or the date.

Retrieving my credit card, I thanked Mary Ann for her help and she went back to the organizing of shelves.

"Come on back," Pat invited, heading for her desk in the rear of the shop. "And speaking of Shirley—how did it work out—her staying with you?"

Obviously she hadn't heard from Shirley.

"Not bad, I *thought*. But she called a cab and took off this morning while I was away having breakfast and thinking she was still asleep. Didn't leave a note or any explanation, so I have no idea why or where she went—home maybe."

Pat shook her head, frowning.

From somewhere out of sight I could hear a regular rhythmic thumping that had grown louder as we neared the back wall.

"What is that sound?" I asked.

"Oh, that's Kelly, our shop production weaver. She's working next door—want to see?"

We walked out a back door into a hallway where through a large window I could see into a room behind the wall of yarns we had left. Kelly was using a large floor loom that I recognized from Rachel Brown's book as a treadle loom.

"It's sometimes called a walking loom," Pat explained, "because of the treadles she's stepping on to raise and lower the harnesses that create the sheds."

"Sure it is," I told her. "Like I really understood those terms—other than *loom*."

She grinned and tried to explain in more simple language.

"The treadles are the long wooden beams she's depressing by stepping back and forth on them to pull down one set of harnesses at a time.

"On this loom there are two sets of harnesses, one set attached individually to every other warp thread, and one to the rest. When Kelly steps on a treadle, all the alternate warp threads are pulled down, leaving the rest up and creating a space between for her to throw across the shuttle that contains the yarn she's using to weave. That space is called a shed. When she releases that treadle and steps on the one connected to the other harnesses, the process is reversed, pulling down the rest of the warp threads to form a different shed—a space in opposition to the previous one. Alternating treadles—and, therefore, sheds—as she throws the shuttle back and forth is what creates the fabric she's weaving."

I nodded wisely, as if I understood and, after watching as Kelly walked the treadles for a few minutes, realized that I did, if a bit simplistically.

The shuttle that held the green yarn with which she was weaving flew quickly back and forth, but the fabric grew slowly, one weft thread at a time, reminding me how laborious it must have been back in the days before machines were invented to do the work. No wonder pioneer women insisted on carrying their looms west in the back of their Conestoga wagons and thereafter spent hours spinning yarn that they used at their looms to make the fabric to clothe their families. After the weaving was done, came the hand sewing to create those items of clothing. I hoped they were appreciated and decided I would never develop a yen to weave enough fabric for anything I intended to wear.

"How much can she weave in, say, an hour?"

"About a yard of simple-weave single-color fabric," Pat told me. "But weaving patterns takes much longer, not including the work of getting the threads ready and warping the loom. It's a lengthy process."

"It's so rhythmic it's almost hypnotic."

"It can be. I've always thought weavers, especially on these big looms, are part mystic. The work becomes automatic, allowing your mind to fall into a kind of meditative state that is a condition of the cadence of the occupation. A few of us sing while we work, as well—or work to music. Keeps the pace even."

In a few minutes we went back to Pat's desk, where we chatted about weaving, then about my traveling in the Winnebago. It made me remember Shirley's disappearance and the article about the dead man in the paper.

Reaching into my bag, I pulled out the front page of the *Taos News* and laid it in front of Pat.

"Did you see this?"

"Oh God, yes! It was all over town before the police had even finished their investigation out at Doris's place. The very idea makes me ill. I can't imagine she'd ever want to use that vat again. But she couldn't anyway—the crime lab people took it, of course."

"Do they know yet who it was she found?"

"Not that I've heard."

We stared at each other, both contemplating the revolting discovery.

"Do you think this Doris had something to do with it?"

"Not a chance. She's a solitary sort who doesn't even come in here often. I think she dyes her own wool not just to get the colors she wants but partly because she's more comfortable at home. It must have been a nasty shock for her, but I doubt she'd ever . . ." She let the sentence trail off.

"But you know her?"

"Sure. She's had a piece in a show or two here."

I hesitated for a second or two, not sure what I was about to ask, or why. "Does Shirley?"

"Know Doris, you mean?"

"Yes."

She stopped shuffling papers on her desk and gave me a sharp, inquisitive look.

"I don't think so. Why?"

Then I felt ridiculous.

"I don't know why," I told her. "It just popped into my head, for no particular reason."

Pat nodded and went back to what she was doing, slowly.

"I'll see you tomorrow night," I told her, knowing she had things to do before the show. Otherwise, I might have shared what Shirley had told me about Tony Cole, to see if Pat knew about the con he had perpetrated, or had any ideas about Shirley's odd behavior.

She looked up again, her eyes narrowed in contemplation.

"There's something about Shirley, isn't there?" she said.

We stared at each other as I nodded. She was right. But neither of us seemed able to get a handle on what that *something* was, so we let it go without another word.

My loom and the other weaving accoutrements were waiting for me on the counter. As I went to claim them, Pat called after me.

"There's a good bluegrass group at the Adobe Bar tonight. I'm going. Would you like to come with me?"

I nodded yes—both because I have a fondness for that kind of music and because I wouldn't mind having a look at the place where Shirley had met Tony. Though what it could tell me, if anything, I had no idea.

"Meet you in the lobby of the Taos Inn at seven?" she suggested.

I agreed, collected my purchases, and headed downtown.

# TWELVE

ON THE MAP OF TAOS I HAD NOTICED THAT THERE WAS A large parking area behind the Moby Dickens Bookshop, and by taking Camino de la Placita, which ran parallel a block west of Paseo del Pueblo, I found my way there and pulled into a space in the shade of a large tree. Knowing the bookstore would probably frown on animals, I left Stretch in the car to wait—and was glad I had when I noticed a cat sitting in a window near the front counter. It was a pleasant shop, packed with books of general interest, as well as a fascinating assortment of local history, and I spent a half hour exploring its literary offerings. Selecting two, one on Mabel Dodge Luhan and another on Colorado, where I meant to go sometime soon, I went upstairs and found the mystery section, where I picked out a third, Margaret Maron's latest, *Rituals of the Season*.

Living in a motor home has its limitations, as well as its benefits. One of the former is lack of space in which to keep books. Admittedly, I am a book collector of the pack rat sort. I like the feel of them, the size and texture of their covers and pages, the smell of print on paper. At home my tall bookshelves full of books of many sizes and colors are better than wallpaper, more vibrant and interesting, full of the promise of new and old friends. Raised by parents who loved books and encouraged reading, I have always had trouble letting go of my books, though the shelves may be full to overflowing into stacks on the floor. During my first trip in a motor home with restricted space I therefore established a rule for myself: For every book I bring into the Winnebago, one must go out—unless—and I do have an escape clause—unless I elect to ship those I cannot bear to part with to a friend in Homer, Alaska, who holds them for me until I eventually come home to claim them.

So, by picking up three new books, I would be honor bound to make decisions concerning which three that were already aboard my rig would not leave Taos with me, one way or an-other. *Later,* I told myself. *I'll decide later, but definitely before I drive out of town.* So, paying for the new ones, I ferried them back to the car, where I left them, took Stretch on his leash, and set out to explore the Taos Plaza.

To reach it, we walked through a parklike area—JOHN DUNN HOUSE SHOPS, a sign told me—with benches that circled shade trees and other plantings, making a pleasant place to stop and sit, if one was so inclined. A few white, yellow, and blue flowers were in bloom and I caught a whiff of a perfume that was vaguely familiar, though I couldn't identify it. Care had been taken in the selection of trees for their color and they made a lovely contrast in dark and light greens, dark plum, and a bright yellow green.

The area was lined on either side by a number of shops and galleries. Some were housed on a second story, accessed by a stair leading up to a covered balcony. The buildings were the usual tan adobe, but rather than the lovely, typical shade of blue I had first noticed at the Kachina Lodge, then on the trim of other places, the woodwork on the stair rails, windows, and doors was, like that of the Apple Tree, painted white—also attractive against the brown of the walls.

Small birds warbled in the branches overhead and flew down to pick at crumbs scattered by a young woman who sat in front of a fabric shop called Common Thread, peeling crusts from the sandwich she was eating to share with feathered appetites. She smiled and nodded as we passed.

Glad to be out of the car, Stretch trotted along in well-behaved fashion, keeping close and pausing only to check out a planter or two as we passed. He paid scant attention to the birds, with only a sidewise glance or two, having learned early that chasing them—like the saucy squirrels we have in Homer—would be fruitless and cost him more dignity than he was willing to sacrifice.

Following a curve in the walkway, we passed between two buildings and came to the southeast corner of the Historic Taos Plaza, where I stopped to take a look before moving on. There again the buildings were the adobe brown, but the trim was the traditional blue that seemed so popular. Most were two stories and full of a variety of shops that surrounded the rectangular square itself, which was about the size of a city block. It was paved, except for one grassy area and planters that held a few shrubs and a number of trees, much older and larger than those in the smaller and newer John Dunn shop area. There were two or three evergreens, but most of the dozen or so were cottonwoods of a smaller-leafed variety different in appearance from those I am used to in Alaska. A number of low walls and benches provided casual seating space for the few people I could see resting there, and several more were walking across from one side of the open plaza to the other.

From a book I had browsed in Moby Dickens, I knew that the plaza had an ancient history even before the first Spaniards visited the place. In 1540, Coronado sent a Captain Alvarado on a reconnaissance party to the north and these Europeans were the first to see the Indians of the Taos Pueblo, which is still in existence north of town, with a population of about nine hundred. The plaza continues to belong to these people, though they have given ownership of the streets that run between the square and its surrounding buildings to the town. At one time the plaza was a trading site for Indians from all around the area.

Watching out for traffic, which moved counterclockwise around the inner square where there was diagonal parking in front of the shops and businesses, I took Stretch across to the middle of the plaza, where I could see everything and decide where to go first. A red-lettered sign on a second story midway down the west side identified the Hotel La Fonda de Taos. At street level I could see an outfitters store, a restaurant, and at least one jewelry shop. To the east were several galleries, a bookstore, what looked like a drugstore, and, at the far end, Noisy Water, whatever that was. Across from it on the northeast corner a sign read CHARLEY'S CORNER, next door to a continuing line of shops and galleries to attract tourists.

Turning south, I noticed on the second floor of the building that took up that whole end of the plaza a patio with tables and chairs for a restaurant I remembered from my map. It was time to recharge the batteries, and Ogelvies Taos Grill & Bar looked like the perfect place to find lunch for myself and watch the people going back and forth in the plaza below. Even better, Stretch would probably be accepted in this outdoor section.

He was, and in ten minutes I was seated at a table with him, on the floor at my feet, charming the friendly waitress who arrived to take my order for soup and half a sandwich to go with a bottle of Dos Equis she had brought with the menu at my request. I'm not much of a beer drinker, but it seemed the right thing to go along with spiced vegetable beef soup.

Between the patio and the street below rose the tops of two or three trees in full bloom, white with a hint of pink. I thought they must be some kind of fruit trees, but had no idea what kind. From where I sat, except for the closest, southeast corner, obscured by the blossoms, I could see over them and down to the square. On a bench near the center a man sat facing me as he read a newspaper. Closer, near the street, two other men stood talking, one of them watching idly as a woman carrying several plastic-bagged purchases passed them, heading across toward the west side. The hum of traffic was steady, but not constant, as cars circled the square looking for a parking place, or pulled away from the curb and were replaced by new arrivals.

I was about to turn away from my perusal of the activity below when I saw a woman step from behind the blossoming trees into the corner of the square and go hurriedly at what was almost a trot toward its center, crossing the space diagonally from southeast to northwest, with slight deviations as she avoided a low wall and two benches. Though she was moving away from me, I thought I recognized the blue denim pantsuit from the day before. Without stopping, she turned halfway round to cast a glance back over a shoulder, as if she expected someone to be following. It *was* Shirley—in yesterday's clothes, including the blue and white blouse she had been wearing when we left the duplex—and she looked either angry or frightened. I couldn't tell which from half a block away, but I could see that she was not happy.

From where I sat I knew there was no way I could leave the patio, go back through the restaurant, down the stairs to the front of the building, and cross the street to the square in time to catch up with her. Knowing this, and not being sure that I wanted to anyway, I sat where I was and watched her reach the far side of the square and cross the street. As she was disappearing around the corner of one of those most distant shops, a male figure came running into my line of sight from behind the cover of the flowering trees. He took the same line as he crossed the square, clearly following her, though from the way she acted, I didn't think she wanted to be caught.

Evidently he had missed seeing where she had gone, for he stopped in the middle and looked carefully around, failed to see her, and clenched a fist that he shook in front of him as he swore an oath I couldn't hear. He walked up to the man on the bench, who lowered his paper and looked up at the interruption to his reading, then shook his head.

His questioner turned away, looked around once more in apparent frustration, and began to walk quickly back the way he had come. I could see as he came closer that he was frowning in irritation.

The waitress arrived with my lunch, and I turned back to see that, having set my soup in front of me, she was looking down into the square and waving. A glance showed me that he had raised his hand to her as he vanished behind the concealing white flowers on his way out of the plaza.

"You know him?" I asked her.

"Oh sure. That's Alan Medina. He runs his family's gallery a little way up Kit Carson Road. You should stop in. They have some great stuff." She gestured in the direction of the street on the southeast corner that led immediately to Paseo del Pueblo, where I remembered the stoplight that backed up traffic in the middle of town. Across the intersection, I had noticed on the map, it turned into Kit Carson Road, which was lined for a couple of blocks with more shops and galleries.

"Anything else I can get for you?" she asked.

Assuring her there was not, I decided to ask no further questions, but ate my soup and sandwich while I considered what I had seen.

Looking down into the square was a little like watching a movie on television with the sound turned off. You could see what was happening, but you had no point of reference to know what it meant.

I had immediately wondered if the man chasing Shirley could be the Tony she said had taken her money, but he was—according to the waitress who evidently knew him—a local, not some businessman from out of town. The impression I had from seeing his dark hair and skin color had made me wonder if he was Indian, but the name she had given, Medina, was Spanish in origin.

Taos was definitely a town of three nationalities—Indian, Spanish, and Anglo—many involved in one way or another with the variety of arts and crafts that defined the community. It was interesting that though the shops and galleries that lined the plaza seemed to be mostly managed by the latter two cultures, the land itself was still owned by the Pueblo Indians, who had never lost it. The idea pleased me, for I knew there were many parts of the Southwest where this was not the case, where the land had simply been taken from the Native peoples and given to immigrants.

Letting it all go, I took Stretch for a walk around the plaza, wandering into a shop or two, finding a lot of tourist kitsch and some very nice pieces of original artwork. Finally, with a rest on one of those benches in the square in mind, I bought a soft drink for myself and an ice cream bar for him. He loves ice cream on a stick, but chocolate is not good for dogs, so I remove that, and half the ice cream, before he gets his licks.

It was growing warm and I had seen enough for the time being, so we went back to the car and then home, stopping briefly at the grocery on the way.

I spent part of the afternoon assembling my student loom, a fairly simple operation given the instructions that came in the box with it. Completed, it stood like an easel on the dinette table and I could see that I would be able to weave a piece about twenty inches long and fifteen inches wide—just right for a cushion cover, if it turned out reasonably well. Following the instructions that came with the loom, I warped it, running the strong neutral thread back and forth between the teeth at the top and bottom. Though I was tempted to take out the yarn I had selected for weaving and give it a try, I thought better of it and decided to wait until Monday afternoon, when Pat could help get me started correctly.

Instead, I took out the mystery I had picked out at Moby Dickens, settled myself on the couch with a glass of iced tea, and got a good start on it. I left the air conditioner off and could hear birds in the tree overhead again and the hum of insects in the long grass outside the fence that surrounded the RV park. By three thirty I found myself rereading paragraphs and pages, so I snoozed a bit before taking Stretch out for a walk.

We circled the perimeter of the grounds. There were few trees, so I felt lucky to have a space in the shade of one. As we walked the lightly graveled dirt road the sun was warm on my shoulders, but I had worn my wide-brimmed straw hat and sunglasses, so I didn't mind, but I noticed the scents of sage and warm earth that drifted past. Living in Alaska you forget the dry, dusty smell of prolonged heat with little rain that is typical in the southern states. What rain does fall often evaporates before reaching the ground. No wonder adobe lasts so long.

A grasshopper flew suddenly out of the brush in front of us, the buzz of its wings causing Stretch to stop and look for the source, but the hopper was already gone.

Back at the Winnebago, I made myself a salad to go with slices from a roast chicken I had picked up at the grocery delicatessen, fed Stretch, and took a quick shower before dressing to meet Pat at the bar in the Taos Inn for our musical evening. Feeling festive, I wore my silver bracelets and earrings, along with a new dress I had found in Santa Fe the previous week. Taking along a sweater in case it was cool later, I was ready to go out the door by six thirty.

"Stay home and be a good galah while I'm gone," I told Stretch, giving him a pat or two. "I won't be late."

Sometimes it's good to tell someone when you'll be back and find him waiting when you are.

I knew that by the time I reached the Adobe Bar he would be curled up under the table, mostly napping but fully prepared to let anyone who was imprudent enough to even walk past outside know that he was ready and able to defend our house on wheels.

# THIRTEEN

THE TAOS INN WAS LOCATED ON PASEO DEL PUEBLO North, a block from the midtown intersection, so I found a place to park on Bent Street and walked the short distance. When Pat came hurrying into the lobby of the inn at just after seven, she found me examining its fountain, which was surrounded by vertical beams that rose up over two stories to support a stained-glass cupola.

"Sorry," she said, a little breathlessly. "I had to park across the street in the lot behind the John Dunn Shops. Bluegrass music is popular around here and I'd forgotten how fast the space out back fills up."

I assured her it was no problem and that actually I had been glad of the time to enjoy the spectacular lobby, which in the 1800s, a brochure had told me, was a small plaza enclosed by adobe houses, with a community well in the center that had eventually been replaced by the fountain and cupola. In the 1890s, the largest of the houses was bought and occupied by Thomas Paul "Doc" Martin, the county's first, and only, physician. He, along with his wife, ultimately purchased the rest of the property. When he died, his wife, Helen, had the plaza enclosed and, in 1936, opened the Hotel Martin—a name that was changed to the Taos Inn by subsequent owners.

The converted adobe houses are today various parts of the hotel. Doc Martin's house became the restaurant, the plaza, the lobby, and Adobe Bar, which was billed as "the living room of Taos" and featured an assortment of live entertainment five nights a week, from bluegrass and flamenco to Celtic, gospel, and folk music. The hotel registration desk was on one side, and the remaining space was filled with seating. But through windows in the west wall I could see that outside, between the main bar and Paseo del Pueblo Norte, was an extension in the form of a patio, with tables at which people settled to enjoy the famous margaritas and watch—the traffic pass along the street—see-and-be-seen. Featured musicians are visible to patrons at both inside and outside tables and their music spills pleasantly through.

As we stood near the desk a talented fiddler began a rousing rendition of "Orange Blossom Special," the kind of music that makes it impossible for me to keep my feet from tapping.

"This is great, but where's Ford?" Pat asked, glancing around the room. "I asked him to save us a couple of places and, with this crowd, I hope he did."

The room was tall and open, and the close-set tables and chairs filled all available space. The walls were white, with several pieces of colorful artwork, and the ceiling around the cupola made of narrow poles laid in attractive patterns. The tables were filled and people stood lining the walls behind them, drinks in hand. Folks sat on the stairs leading up to a balcony over the registration desk, where others occupied more tables and leaned over the railing to watch the musicians. Hung over that long balcony rail were several colorful, handwoven rugs similar to those I had seen at Weaving Southwest.

The group of five musicians had set up against one wall. The fiddler was a woman with red hair that glowed like copper from an overhead spotlight and whose fingers were a blur of motion on the strings from which her bow drew the complicated music. Everyone in the room seemed to be in motion as they stomped and clapped so enthusiastically that I could feel the rhythm through the soles of my feet, infectious and lively.

As Pat hesitated, looking around, from the other side of the room I saw a hand waving a signal and caught sight of Ford Whitaker motioning us over.

"There," I said, laying a hand on her shoulder and pointing in his direction.

We made our way through the crowd and, true to his word, though I don't know how he had managed, Ford was holding two chairs for us in a group with five or six other people who were sitting around two small cocktail tables that they had pushed together.

"Hey," he said, when the piece and following applause had ended and it was possible to hear. "Glad you got here. I've had to fend off half a dozen attempts to grab these seats."

"Sorry," Pat told him, and explained her parking problem.

I was introduced to those around the table before a waitress appeared and we ordered margaritas, which arrived in good order, along with a refill for Ford in thanks for saving our places.

There was little opportunity for conversation as the music and enthusiastic appreciation of it by the crowd continued for the next half hour. I was sitting next to Ford and between musical numbers he leaned close to quietly ask me about Shirley.

"I hear you and Pat got her sprung from the hospital and she went home with you yesterday. How's she doing?"

I explained how she had disappeared that morning without a word, leaving me to wonder where and why she left so abruptly, and how I had seen her later in the plaza.

He frowned and shook his head. "That's odd. Did she say anything about what happened?"

"Just—adamantly—that she didn't try to kill herself and didn't know how she got to the garage where her landlady found her. She talked a little about the guy she was seeing. Did you know him—someone named Tony?"

"Not really. I'd met him once—here, I think—but I'd seen them together a time or two. Why? Something wrong there?"

I was deciding what to answer when the music started again, so all I could do was shrug, helpless against the volume.

Ford grinned and nodded. "Later," he mouthed and turned to listen.

After another half hour of music, thinking that it must be about time for the group to take a break, I resolved to beat the crowd to the restroom, got up, and started to make my way across to the door on the far side. I had almost reached it when I caught sight of a totally unexpected and familiar face near a group of people who had not been able to find seats and were standing to listen.

Tall and angular, still wide through the shoulders, narrow at the hips, wearing, as usual, jeans, Western shirt, and well-worn boots, Butch Stringer leaned against the wall, nodding in time to the music. It brought me to a halt so sudden that I attracted his attention and as recognition dawned his whole face lit up with a delighted grin.

"Maxie McNabb!" he crowed and, stepping away from the wall, swept me into a bear hug of greeting that all but took me off my feet. "Where the hell did *you* spring from?"

The last time I had seen the long-distance trucker was a couple of years earlier on the Alaska Highway in a place called Liard River Hot Springs, between Steamboat and Watson Lake, halfway up the long road north. Later the same day, trying to avoid a collision with a passenger car and a pickup towing a boat, Butch had purposely driven his Peterbilt and trailer rig off the highway and been badly injured as a utility pole caved in the front of his cab, breaking both his legs and several ribs. It had been a horrific accident in which four people in the other two vehicles had died. Rescuers had been forced to cut Butch out of his crushed tractor, then medevaced him to a Canadian hospital by helicopter in order to save his life. From there, once stabilized, he had been moved to a hospital in Seattle. After that I lost track of him and, with no way of knowing where or how to make contact, I had finally given up trying and simply hoped he was and would be okay.

Some prayers are answered, it seems, for there he was, alive and well, now holding me off at arm's length and grinning from ear to ear in satisfaction.

"Let's get out of here," he said. "It's good music, but too damn noisy to talk."

I agreed and he led the way through the crowd at the door.

Once outside, however, I suddenly remembered Pat and Ford, who would wonder when I didn't return to the table.

"Wait a second," I told Butch and made a quick trip to explain that I had just met an old friend.

"See you tomorrow night at the show, then," Pat said, and I went back across the room.

Butch stepped out to meet me and I saw that he was limping noticeably.

He saw me looking and nodded toward his left leg, knowing I was acquainted with the history of the injury. "It's nothing now. I got real lucky, considering the mess they were both in before surgery. They thought for a while I'd lose this one, but I had a stubborn doc who got me through still standing on my own pegs."

"Is it painful?"

"Oh, it kicks up a bit when it rains." He grinned. "But it doesn't rain that often in New Mexico. Took me out of a truck, though."

I could imagine that it would, remembering that he had been making regular trips of over 2,600 miles from Seattle to Anchorage and that driving 80,000 pounds of truck and trailer for ten hours or five hundred miles a day would be more stress than his kind of injuries could endure.

"Do you miss it?"

"Yeah, but not half as much as I would have missed the leg."

It was, I agreed, a more than fair exchange, though regrettable. Before the accident I had had the opportunity to watch him maneuver his huge rig with the confidence and assurance of an expert and knew he had been very good at what he did.

"Things happen and you change directions," he said, with a dismissive lift of those broad shoulders, and switched gears. "Have you had dinner?"

"Yes, but not dessert," I told him. "You?"

"I should have a table in the dining room right about now. Join me?"

I did and, after that quick trip to the restroom, was soon rewarded with a flan from the dessert menu, while Butch started on his pork tenderloin, served with a baked yam, glazed carrots, and some kind of salsa.

"I treat myself once a month to dinner at Doc's," he told me. "Drive up from Santa Fe and take advantage of good food *and* good music."

"So you're not living here?"

"No, I moved to Santa Fe as soon as my busted ribs healed up and they had done all they could for my legs—almost a year ago. I'm running the office for a trucking company down there and do a little driving on short, in-state runs once in a while to keep my hand in. We've got a good bunch of distance guys—and a few gals—and I like the country.

"But tell me what you're doing in Taos. It's a long way from Alaska. Vacation? For how long? Are you still driving that motor home? And I want to know what happened after the accident. Did you catch up with Jessie? And how about the boy?"

So I told him how I had wound up in Taos after my friend Sarah died in Grand Junction. How open-ended my travels were and that I hadn't decided where I would go next in the Winnebago—maybe back to Homer for a month or two, but maybe not. That I was thinking of driving east to parts of the country I had never seen, but planned to be in Taos for the next couple of weeks at least.

Then I related the part of the story of my trip up the highway with Jessie Arnold that he had missed, and that the boy, Patrick, was fine and living in Fairbanks.

"That Jessie," he said, remembering with a smile. "She's a pistol, that one. And that husky of hers . . . What was his name?"

"Tank."

"Right. Your two dogs really got along, didn't they? Do you still have Stretch?"

I assured him that I did—though at times I think it's the other way around and Stretch really has me.

As we talked I had examined his face and noticed that the accident and recovery had left their mark there, as well as on his legs. There were a few more lines and a slightly heavy look around his eyes, of the sort that I've noticed before in people who have experienced extended periods of pain and struggle, physical or mental. My Daniel, for one, who suffered the agony of a cancer undetected until too late to do anything but help him die in as little pain as possible, which was not easy toward the end. But there had been and still was something intrinsically fine about Butch, something that made him the kind of person one likes to have as a friend, who doesn't do anything by halves. I could see that the new lines in his face could not all be attributed to his accident, that many were the kind that result from smiles like the one with which he had greeted me.

"You know," he said slowly, pushing his empty plate to one side and nodding to the waiter, who asked if he wanted coffee before he took it away, "the one thing I've missed in living down here for most of a year is all the people I know back on the coast. It's hard to start all over in a new place, when you spent most of your life somewhere else and don't know anyone. Don't you miss the old friends you have in Homer?"

It was a trade-off that I had anticipated and made peace with before I took off to play gypsy in my motor home, but still, once in a while, I do feel the lack of enduring friendships with people who know me well and vice versa, and told him so.

"I felt very lonesome after Sarah died last fall in Grand

Junction, but in that case I would have felt the same if I'd gone home to Alaska.

"I do go back at least once a year for two or three months, and that helps me keep in touch. Once in a while a friend, or my son, Joe, shows up and travels with me for a week or two."

"Well," Butch said, smiling again, "you're here now and I don't intend to lose track of you again, or let you get away with just one evening of catching up. I'm here for the weekend, so let's spend some time in the next couple of days and enjoy each other's company without chasing bad guys up a highway. Okay?"

"More than okay."

The idea certainly appealed to me, so I agreed readily. How could I have guessed that the part about the bad guys might turn out the other way around?

But the evening was still young, so I invited him to come back with me to the Winnebago and say hello to Stretch.

"It's a lot less crowded and quieter there. Besides, I have a bottle of Jameson that, for all I know, could be going bad for lack of interest."

"Great! My pickup's parked out back. How about if I drive you to your car, then follow you to this RV park?"

# FOURTEEN

EARLIER ANOTHER GORGEOUS SUNSET HAD SPREAD ITSELF out across the western sky as I drove into downtown Taos to meet Pat, so it was full dark when Butch and I arrived at the Winnebago at nine thirty. The rig was dark, though I thought I had left a light on as usual for Stretch. But, with my attention on the brilliant colors, it was possible that I had forgotten it.

When I put my key in the coach door it wouldn't turn to unlock the door, and it took me a moment to realize that it wasn't locked. That made me hesitate, for I might overlook a light, but never to lock up tight when I'm leaving, even for a few minutes' walk and coming quickly back.

"Something wrong?" Butch asked, noticing my uncertainty.

"The door's open. I must have neglected to lock it when I left—but I never do that, especially when I leave Stretch alone."

"Hey," he said, as I started to open the door. "Let me go first—just in case, okay? Where's the light switch?"

"On the wall just inside the door."

He found the switch, flipped it, and we were met with total chaos.

One thing I quickly learned on my first trip in the motor home is that clutter seems to accumulate much faster than it does in the larger area of a house. I am very visual, so much so that I have to admit that in terms of a possession, if I can't see it I might as well not own it. But I can't leave things lying around everywhere in the Winnebago, so I have trained myself to establish specific places for things and put them there when I'm not using them. As we stepped in and looked around I realized that I might as well not have taken the trouble, for the interior that I had left neatly in order was a total shambles and what appeared to be everything I owned was now scattered in plain sight.

Cupboards stood open and partially empty, much of their contents now littering the countertops or the floor—dishes, pots, and pans mixed with boxes and cans of food items. The refrigerator door was propped open by a gaping crisper drawer, what it had held dumped onto the floor—vegetables, fruit, a package of cheese, a jar of pickles, and other food containers. The freezer had been similarly emptied, including a container of ice cream that was melting in an ever-widening circle. The cushions for the benches of the dinette had been thrown onto the sofa and the bedding stored inside each bench pulled out and cast aside—luckily far from the ice cream.

The storage compartment over the cab was open and empty of books and videos, which lay scattered as if hastily tossed over a shoulder, though the television and video player were still there.

I turned to look down the passageway to the bedroom and could see that the closet doors stood open and items which had been stored within both them and the adjoining drawers had been dumped onto the floor or bed, from which the sheets, blankets, and pillows had been pulled as well.

The more I looked, the angrier I became.

"Good God!" Butch said. "I'd say you've had a burglar, Maxie—someone who worked hard to thoroughly search this rig for something valuable."

Then for a moment I panicked, realizing I did not see Stretch anywhere in the confusion—or his footprints, for that matter. Then I realized that I could hear, and had been hearing, his familiar barks and whines from somewhere close at hand—behind the closed door of the lavatory.

Taking a wide step over the mess in front of the refrigerator, I opened the lavatory door to find him covered with laundry detergent from a box that had been spilled onto the floor, along with other cleaning items that I keep in the under-sink storage cupboard. Mixed among these were my toothbrush, toothpaste tube, a container of Tylenol, and other medical items from the over-sink cabinet. It wasn't surprising that he greeted me with a sneeze.

"Had a bad time, lovie?" I asked him, relieved, and carried him back to where Butch stood waiting with a smile.

"Hey there, buddy. You okay?" he said, and reached to give him a pat.

Stretch showed his teeth and growled, a thing he almost never does. But it had been a long time since he had briefly met Butch on the road to Alaska, and it had clearly had been a tempestuous and confusing evening, full of at least one, probably unfriendly, stranger. This, as far as he was concerned, was another. I couldn't blame him. Neither did Butch.

"I think you should call the police," he said.

"My thoughts exactly."

I made use of my cell phone and, while we waited for law enforcement to show up, attempted to figure out if anything had been stolen, first checking my camera equipment and laptop computer, the two most obvious things in which a thief would be interested. Neither was missing, though everything in the camera bag had been dumped out onto the floor beside the closet and the computer lay where it had been tossed onto the bare mattress. I couldn't see that anything was gone. It was more as if whoever had made a wreck of my living quarters had been searching for something specific and cast aside anything that didn't fit the description of whatever it was.

Drawers of clothing had been searched, as had the drawer where I keep my costume jewelry and the odds and ends I have collected.

A glance had told me my secret compartment had remained secret, so there would be no need to reveal its presence, add a missing shotgun to a police report, or the small amount of cash—two hundred dollars at most—that lay hidden with it.

"You know," Butch said, as we waited outside, "driving in, I noticed another motor home or two, one with lights on. I think I'll go ask if they heard or saw anything suspicious."

"Good idea," I agreed. "I'll get Stretch cleaned up and wait here. I shouldn't think the police will be long."

They weren't.

Two uniformed officers pulled up in a squad car ten minutes later, as I had just finished rinsing Stretch clean of laundry soap with the outside sprayer and wrapped him in a towel to dry off.

The taller, younger, Anglo officer—introduced as Taylor— clearly of lesser rank, occupied himself in filling out a form on the specifics of the Winnebago, its registration, and my driver's license and seemed willing to let his partner do most of the talking while he took notes.

"Well," said Officer Herrera, older, and shorter, with eyes so dark brown I thought at first they were black. From the wrinkles around them I assumed his most usual expression was a smile, but now he was frowning at the turmoil that was evident inside. "This is a first. As far as I know we've never had a break-in that involved a motor home. Looks like a pretty thorough job of going through everything you own. When did you find it?"

I told him that and where I had been earlier.

"And you say you found the door unlocked?"

"Yes."

"There are no broken windows and the door wasn't jimmied, so your burglar either had the tools to open a cab door— they're both unlocked—or had a key. Have you given a key to anyone?"

I had not. But I immediately thought of Shirley. I had meant to give her the extra one, if she had stayed. Going to the cupboard where I keep it, I found the hook empty, though I knew the key had been there when I arrived in Taos, for I had seen it. Would she have taken it when she disappeared? I had no way of knowing when it had gone missing, so I let the suspicion slide, hesitant to accuse her. She had left the door unlocked when she took off, hadn't she? Wouldn't she have locked it if she'd had the means to do so?

We had stepped back outside, and both men swung around at the sound of Butch's approach on the gravel of the drive, but relaxed when I explained his presence as a friend and where he had been.

"Those people notice anything?" the officer asked.

"They heard a vehicle, but assumed it was a resident so they didn't bother to look. They said that from the sound of the engine it might have been a pickup rather than a car."

"We'll talk to them before we leave."

The two of them spent close to half an hour examining the inside of the Winnebago, dusting for fingerprints, taking Butch's and mine for comparison, talking to my neighbors, and then were gone, with my signature on the report.

"With nothing stolen, there's not much we can do," the first officer told me before they left. "We'll run the prints we lifted through AFIS, but, from the look of the smudges, I think whoever it was wore gloves. We'll let you know, Ms. McNabb. You said you'd be here for a couple of weeks, right?"

Left alone with the mess, Butch and I spent the better part of an hour clearing and cleaning it. I wiped away fingerprint powder from everywhere I could find it and reorganized the galley while he sorted out the bathroom, then helped me remake the bed—a much easier task with two people, one to each side. The whole job actually didn't take long. There simply isn't that much in a motor home, though it had first appeared to be a lot. A certain amount of the refrigerator's contents had to be discarded, including that puddle of ice cream, but the place was soon acceptably neat again, so we rewarded ourselves with some of the Jameson I had promised as we left the Taos Inn.

Stretch had stopped growling and accepted Butch's presence. When he sat down on the couch, glass in hand, Stretch followed, wagging his tail in seeming apology for the earlier display of bad temper, and sat down at Butch's feet in typical friendly fashion.

Like most everyone to whom Stretch appeals, Butch could not resist reaching down to rub those floppy velvet ears and give his back a pat. Without an invitation, he jumped up beside the man and lay down against his leg, correctly assuming a welcome.

The dog is no dummy, but neither is Butch.

"You're a good boy," he told Stretch, continuing his ministrations, "but you think you've got the whole world fooled, don't you?"

"I'm just glad he wasn't hurt," I told him. "Rather than shutting him in the bathroom, whoever was in here could just as easily have hit him with something, or kicked him outside. He thinks he's a Rottweiler, you know. He must have been pretty scared and angry at the intrusion, or he'd never have growled at you when you came in with me."

I thought about that later, when Butch had gone, after making sure I had securely locked every door and closed every window, curtain, and blind in precaution. Though I couldn't help thinking it was like closing the door on an empty barn, but if it made him feel better, it was all right with me. I opened the ceiling vents as soon as I was alone, however, not able to stand being all but hermetically sealed into the space.

Left to myself, I had to admit I felt a little shaky about someone breaking into my residence, even if it was on wheels. What could he or they—I realized it could have been more than one, though for some reason I doubted it—have been looking for? If he'd wanted something salable, why hadn't he grabbed my computer and cameras?

I made myself a cup of tea, got ready for bed, and climbed in with a book that I soon laid aside, realizing I was totally unable to concentrate on fiction when I had an actual mystery of my own too near at hand and mind for comfort.

Stretch was keeping very close, and once or twice had stopped to listen attentively to ordinary sounds from outside that he normally would have ignored. So I took pity and lifted him up and let him curl up next to me, where he soon settled and was napping. It would be a good idea, I told myself, to let him stay there for the night to regain his self-assurance, though he usually sleeps in his own basket on the floor next to the bed. I was feeling more than a little vulnerable myself and his presence was welcome.

It is remarkable how threatened an intrusion into your private space makes you feel. We go along, day to day, assuming we are safe and ignoring how easy it would be for someone to just walk right in, invited or not, with good or bad intentions. When someone does, it shakes all your confidence in being safe behind locked doors. I couldn't help wondering what would have happened if I had been at home and was glad I had not been.

I was also glad to have had Butch with me when I tried to open the door. Now that he was gone I found myself feeling very much alone, and had an odd compulsion to pick up the phone and call someone, which is what I would have done if I had been at home. But I couldn't think of anyone in particular I wanted to talk to except perhaps my son, Joe. I decided against it, though. Why call someone just to tell them you've been burglarized, when there's nothing they can do long distance but worry? I knew what my daughter's response would be, considering that Carol and her husband, Philip, both heartily objected to my traveling lifestyle already. A break-in would just add another string to their bow of disapproval— another reason to once again suggest that I should move in-to an old-folks' home and let them manage my life—and finances.

"Not bloody likely," I said out loud, and Stretch opened his eyes to give me a questioning look. "I'm just fine on my own, like it or not. Aren't I, you darlin' dog?"

Like the Indian in *The Last of the Mohicans,* I am the last, not of my tribe but of my family. I was the youngest. My par-ents are long gone and both my brother and my sister have passed, like my two husbands. After being raised in a family of five, who were close, exuberant, and anything but silent or shy about making their opinions heard, I always find that my first instinct is to share, good news or bad. I miss my siblings, espe-cially the brother who was closest to me in age, but also my older sister, Phyllis.

I forced my thoughts elsewhere—how glad I was to have run into Butch Stringer again and to know he had come out of the accident on the way to Alaska in better shape than might have been the case. He was such a fine and honest person, with a good sense of humor and a positive appreciation of life, the kind of person you instinctively know you can trust in any-thing he says or does. Meeting him was like falling back into step with a familiar and cherished acquaintance. Each of you automatically and without conscious effort adjusts your stride to the other's and your conversation as well.

I was glad that before he left he had suggested that we go for a drive the next day.

"I'd like to take a look at the Rio Grande Gorge Bridge," he had told me.

I had agreed, if I could take Stretch along. It would be good to get out of town, even just a few miles out, and we would both enjoy his company.

Feeling better, I shut off the light, rolled over, gave Stretch a pat to let him know he could stay, and went to sleep refusing to allow myself to rethink the events of the evening again.

I don't often dream of my Daniel, so I treasure it when I do.

Sometime in the early hours of that Friday morning I found myself in familiar resistance to waking, somehow knowing it would be bittersweet when I did—which, of course, confirmed that it already was. Keeping my eyes shut, struggling to retain the reality of my dream, as always I felt its precious detail slip away, much as the brilliant colors of a sunset fade into pastels before they disappear. The longer you try to hold on to a dream the less you can recall.

I knew we had been walking together along a road in Homer, for I remembered a view of the bay and the mountains of the Kenai Range rising majestically beyond it to the south. It was a thing we had done often and I had valued those walks for their peace and what it said about our relationship. Couples who have long been close walk together differently than those who have not—steadily and in step, a sort of unspoken affirmation. We had been walking like that, holding hands, and whatever small speech we had made had been pleasant and positive.

Then, as usual, the images were gone with Daniel, but I had no trouble retaining the emotion—a gift as dear as it had been when he was alive and we really had walked that road. Eyes still closed, I clung to that feeling as I gave up, let the rest go, and, grateful for small treasures, resettled myself in the bed.

Stretch shifted his weight near my feet and we both went back to sleep.

# FIFTEEN

OFFICER HERRERA ARRIVED ALONE THE NEXT MORNING about nine, an hour before Butch was scheduled to appear.

"G'morning, Ms. McNabb," he greeted me through the screen door, which I had locked, though I had left the solid door open. "Are you okay after last night?"

I assured him I was and invited him in for coffee, which he accepted with a smile, laying a handful of paperwork on the table beside his cup.

"I have some information I wanted to check with you," he said, after he had added two spoonfuls of sugar but no cream to his brew. "We got a hit on the fingerprints."

"That was pretty fast, wasn't it?"

I had always thought it took hours, even days, for a computerized search of the national bank of fingerprints.

"Well—things are a bit slow right now and this is an interesting case. So when I got back to the station and found the system wasn't busy I entered the prints we found that didn't belong to you or Mr. Stringer and left it to search overnight.

This morning I found we had a positive result on several of them, for the same individual—a woman."

*Shirley*, I immediately assumed, considering that she was the only other female who had been inside the Winnebago since my arrival in Taos.

"Do you know a Sharon Beil? Has she, to your knowledge, been in here in the last few days?"

"No, never heard of her. Is that who was in here last night tearing things apart?"

"Ah . . ." He hesitated, frowning. "Maybe, but those prints were mixed with the smudges we found—they overlapped each other. But you say you don't know her, so for now we'll assume that it was. I'm thinking there were probably two people involved last night."

"Who is this Sharon Beil?"

"A woman arrested in California three years ago on a shoplifting charge—a pretty minor incident."

"And did you find any unidentified prints from another woman?" I asked. "A friend did stay over night before last."

"No one else."

I knew that I had given the whole motor home a complete spring cleaning before leaving Arizona, and no one but Shirley, whoever had broken in the night before, and Butch had been inside since then. So why wouldn't the police have found Shirley's prints as well? Had she been careful what she touched and removed them before she left so abruptly? Could she *be* this Sharon Beil person simply using Shirley Martin as an alias? What the hell was going on?

"I've put out a statewide alert for Sharon Beil," Officer Herrera told me.

"Do you have a picture?"

He fished a computer printout from his thin pile of papers and handed it across the table to me.

I sat staring down at the police photo of a woman—*Shirley!* Or was it? The longer I studied it, the less sure I was—but it was close. The woman's hair was brown and she seemed slightly heavier, a little older, but—with a face-lift and a bleach job? No, maybe not. The bone structure of the face seemed fuller and longer.

"You know her?" he asked, leaning forward attentively.

I shook my head finally.

"I can't say absolutely, but I don't think this is my friend— well, she's not exactly a friend, just an acquaintance who stayed here with me for one night. I think it's not her, but it's so similar that for a minute I thought it was."

"You're sure?"

"Ah—no, I'm not. But I don't think so. When was this picture taken?"

"Four years ago. What's your friend's name?"

I told him and he wrote it down, along with the address of the duplex, which I hoped would not cause Shirley problems if she was not involved. It would certainly not be to the liking of her landlady, Ann, to have the police show up looking for her tenant. Still, the resemblance bothered me.

Could Shirley have changed so much? It was possible. Maybe she had had surgery done, bleached her hair, and lost weight since then. Still . . .

"Well, let's see if we have any success in finding this woman, locally or maybe in Santa Fe—or both women, if that's the case. People sometimes look different in person than they do in a mug shot. I'll get back to you, but if you see her again let me know, okay? And, yes, you can keep the picture. It's a copy."

I promised that I would, thinking that perhaps it was time I made an attempt to track Shirley down—if she *was* a Shirley and not a Sharon. I still wasn't sure of that face in the picture. But underneath it all lay a feeling that she either had something to do with the chaos of my living space or would know who did.

Butch drove in as Herrera drove out.

Stepping in the door, he was immediately greeted enthusiastically by Stretch, as if he were still making up for his show of teeth and the growl of the night before.

"Hey there, buster." Butch knelt on the top step to give him the attention demanded and it was a long minute or two before he turned back to me.

"I saw a squad car leaving. Anything new?" he asked, getting up.

As I poured him the last of the coffee, I told him what Herrera had reported.

"She looks kind of familiar," he said, leaning both elbows on the table and frowning thoughtfully at the face in the picture. "I think I've seen this woman somewhere here in town, but not on this trip. Or else I've seen your friend, if this isn't her."

I told him what Pat had said about Shirley's visits to the Adobe Bar and he agreed that it was possible he had seen her there.

Thinking about Pat brought to mind the reception for the weaving show that evening at Weaving Southwest, so I asked Butch if he would like to go. He accepted and suggested that we have dinner afterward, a plan that was definitely to my liking.

"But let's get going before it heats up." He drained his coffee mug and got up to set it in the galley.

We made sure the Winnebago was locked up tight, climbed into Butch's green pickup, and were soon headed north on Paseo del Pueblo, with Stretch resting comfortably on my lap. At the far end, near the Kachina Inn, the street made a wide left turn and became a highway, and in five or six miles we arrived at an intersection with a full set of traffic lights.

"You know," Butch told me with a grin, when we had made another left turn and were traveling on Highway 64, "when I asked for directions to the gorge at the hotel, they told me to follow Paseo del Pueblo until I reached 'the old blinking light' and showed me on a map. That's how it's marked: 'The Old Blinking Light.' It's evidently been a local landmark for years and even though its single blinking traffic light is now history they still call it that. It almost gives a new meaning to the term *three on red*."

"What's that?"

"Well, locals seem to think that you should be able to get three cars through an intersection after the light turns red. Now that's laid-back in my book. There are a lot of laid-back things I like about this town. When and if I ever retire, I might just move here."

"It gets cold in the winter," I reminded him. "Lots of snow and freezing temperatures. Wouldn't it bother your leg?"

"Yeah, but we get snow in Santa Fe too, and if I didn't have to go back and forth to work every day, it wouldn't be much of a problem. I refuse to let a gimp leg get the best of me to the point of making me live somewhere I don't like. Small towns appeal to me. I like this place and its people—a lot."

So did I. I enjoy warm weather, but the idea of snowy winters was attractive as well, considering all the years I've had in Alaska to feel at home in them. I don't think I could settle for the rest of my life in a place like Phoenix where Christmas has no snow. It just wouldn't feel right.

We drove a few miles farther through broad open space of low rolling hills and mesas that rose up west of Taos, and it gradually turned to dry, brush-covered land that reminded me of much of the Four Corners country with its high desert and the area between Grand Junction and Salt Lake through which I had driven the previous fall. I could smell sage through the open window. A magpie perched on a fence post we passed and there were hawks riding thermals overhead against the brilliant blue of the sky. There is less oxygen in the air at almost seven thousand feet elevation, which accounts for the deeper color of the sky and its sunsets.

We couldn't see the Rio Grande Gorge until we were all but upon it. Then, suddenly, we could see the railings of the two-thousand-foot-long bridge that spanned it, but there was nothing higher than those railings to interfere with the flat expanse of the surrounding country. It was a graceful bridge in form— metal girders with a pleasing curve to the central arch that met a shorter one on either end. They rested on a pair of concrete piers that rose up out of the gorge, one on each side of the river that flowed between them.

Butch swung into a parking lot on the eastern side and we walked out onto the bridge and looked down at what seemed a heavy thread of water six hundred and fifty feet below.

The power of water to carve its way into the earth always amazes me. Given sufficient time, following the path of least resistance, the relentless erosion of water can slice its way through even the hardest of stone—the volcanic basalt of northern New Mexico, for instance. How long, I wondered, staring down, had it taken this water to wear its way six hundred and fifty feet down, becoming a river in the process and creating the gorge that fell away below us?

The river was not as large as I had anticipated, but confinement within the narrow gorge had something to do with it—and that I had probably seen too many Western movies of cowboys driving herds of cattle across a wider, shallower river that was always pictured as the Rio Grande and probably was somewhere farther south. It was, in fact, so far down that being there felt almost unreal and that dizzy feeling you sometimes get in looking down from a great height was somehow lessened. Still, I knew it would make anyone who was afraid of heights very nervous indeed, especially when the bridge vibrated slightly as vehicles passed over it. The water of the river was not clear, but a muddy caramel brown. The dark walls of the gorge rose over it in huge steps, revealing the volcanic flows that had formed them, one layer after another, all of which the water had worn through and conquered. Fallen stones lay in piles at the bottom, partially covered with the contrasting soft green of sage, rabbitbrush, and willow.

As we leaned there on the rail, watching, a bright bit of blue in the brown water caught my attention as, around the bend, perhaps half a mile away, an inflatable raft came floating. There were several people in it, and the sight finally gave me some perspective on the depth of the gorge, for they seemed very small in a raft that appeared to be only an inch or two long. What had looked like gravel on the riverbank now could be seen to be huge boulders in contrast.

"That's a long drop," Butch commented, when we had watched the raft float slowly closer, its passengers waving up at us, and finally pass out of sight under the bridge.

We walked back to the pickup and drove across the bridge to a roadside stop on the other side with restrooms and roofed-over picnic tables. There was parking for hikers who elected to go off and clamber down into the gorge somewhere farther south. Such hiking tempted me not at all, but I picked a large handful of sage to take home with me, disturbing a small, swift lizard that scampered off leaving a trail of tiny, neat footprints in the dust.

"Lunch?" Butch asked, when we were almost back to town.

"Let's get back together this evening," I said, begging off. "The reception at Weaving Southwest starts at seven. Let's go about then, okay? I've got an errand or two to run. Then I might just take a nap through the warmest part of the afternoon."

We agreed that he would pick me up about seven and we'd have dinner later. I thanked him for the trip to the gorge and waved as he drove out of the RV park, still pleased that our paths had finally crossed again and thinking I should let our friend Jessie know that I had seen him and he was doing well.

A nap *was* appealing, but I had a couple of other objectives first: a visit to Shirley's landlady, for one, and a conversation with Alan Medina at his gallery on Kit Carson Road, for another. Through them I might be able to somehow catch up with Shirley and get a few answers to the questions that were cluttering my mind—including whether or not she was, or was related to, the woman in the picture that Officer Herrera had given me.

Before total frustration set in, it was time to find out anything I could from the only sources I had.

# Sixteen

I took Stretch along but, remembering the land-lady's reaction to him on our last visit, left him in the car when I reached the duplex Shirley shared with Ann Barnes. As I parked in front I could see that the drapes were closed, as was the garage door, so I couldn't tell if Shirley was there, but knocking on the front door brought no response.

I knew the other half was occupied, however, for I saw a curtain twitch as Ann peered out to see who was stopping by. She was, as I expected, the sort to keep careful track of all her neighbor's comings and goings, and of Shirley's visitors as well. No wonder she had been the one to hear a car running in a closed garage on the other end of the building in the middle of the night. She was also the only person I knew who had actually met Anthony Cole and might be able to tell me something about him.

She kept me waiting on the front step—not showing up to open the door until I had knocked twice, and then trying to look surprised to see me.

"Oh," she said. "Mrs. McNabb, isn't it?"

I think I mentioned she was big on *oh*.

"Yes. I'd like to have a word with you, Mrs. Barnes."

"Oh, I don't know." She took a step back and narrowed the opening of the door with one hand as if she were about to close it. "I'm really very busy at the moment."

"It won't take more than a couple of minutes," I promised, stepping forward onto the doorsill.

As I invaded her comfort zone she backed away, as I'd expected she would. Most people, Americans at least, have an instinctive reluctance to being crowded that can be useful at times.

"Well—all right, but only for a minute or two. I really must . . ."

She allowed the sentence to trail off as she turned and led me into a living room that was an exact reverse copy of Shirley's, but shape was as far as the similarity went.

Almost every surface I could see held something.

The walls were filled with the embroidered mottoes Shirley had mentioned—large and small, framed and on pillows. LIVE EVERY DAY AS IF IT WERE YOUR LAST—TO THINE OWN SELF BE TRUE—BEAUTY IS ONLY SKIN-DEEP—HASTE MAKES WASTE—those were only a few, but I quit reading at that point, wondering if Ann had picked them for what they said or was just compelled to do needlework.

The furniture was covered—tables, chairs, the sofa, even the shelves of a bookcase—with antimacassars and bits of bric-a-brac—bone china cups and saucers on shelves, porcelain figurines—the floors, carpeted or not, with throw rugs. Even her grandfather clock had a dust ruffle.

It was a truly amazing sight, almost awe-inspiring—and very sad. The woman must have had years of time by herself,

with little else to do. I began to understand how having a tenant next door whose life she could vicariously share had become
her obsessive focus.

"Oh," I said.

"You like the mottoes?" she asked, with a smile. "I'll make
you one, if you like."

*Oh damn*, I thought, thinking it would probably read,
BIRDS IN THEIR LITTLE NESTS AGREE.

"It's very kind of you to offer," I told her, "but I travel in a
motor home and not only is space limited, but there's no way to
put a nail in the wall to hold one."

"I could do a pillow."

"Thanks," I said, thinking fast in desperation, "but I've
more of those than I need. You could help more by telling me
a few things about Shirley Morgan."

"Oh, I don't know much about her," Ann said quickly. "I
make it a rule to stay out of the lives of my tenants, you see."

*Sure you do*, I thought. *And if my granny had wheels she'd be
a bicycle.* Now there was a motto that might be useful.

"Have you seen her since yesterday? Was she here last night?"

"How would I know that?" she asked stiffly, determined to
maintain a detached pose.

"When I was here with Shirley you said you had heard water running."

"Oh, well—yes. I suppose I have heard it from time to
time."

"So—have you heard it running yesterday, or today?"

"I might have, I guess. I don't pay much attention."

*In a pig's eye!*

Getting any information out of the woman was like playing
hide-and-go-seek blindfolded.

"Look," I told her somewhat sternly, "Shirley stayed with me night before last, but left without telling me where she was going and hasn't been back since yesterday morning. I'm trying to find her, to make sure she's okay. Can you help me? Or should I call the police and tell them she's missing? They'd probably show up and leave fingerprint powder all over her half of this duplex. Tough to clean up—fingerprint powder—you know?"

That got her attention.

"Oh dear," she said with a frown. "All right. Shirley came back yesterday morning in a taxi. Water was running over there and I heard her talking to some guy on the phone before she left."

How, I wondered, had Ann been able to tell who Shirley had been talking to, or even hear her, for that matter? I didn't ask.

"What makes you think she left?"

"I went to the grocery store and came back just before noon. She must have left while I was gone, because I haven't seen or heard anything else—yesterday or today. Maybe she found another place."

"Let's go and find out. You've got a key, right?"

"Oh, I don't think so," she said, shaking her head. "It's not legal for me to go in without notice."

Bicycle-granny wheeled through my mind again.

"Look," I told her, "you didn't see her leave. You're just assuming she did. Supposedly she tried to commit suicide once already. Don't you think she could have made another attempt, a quieter one this time that didn't involve carbon monoxide? I think we have enough of a reason to find out, don't you?"

She stared at me, eyes wide. Then she turned without a word and went into her kitchen. I heard a cabinet door open and close, and she came back with a key in her hand.

As we went across to the front door of Shirley's half of the duplex I noticed that Ann was not using the cane she had carried when we met. Evidently, she either had good days when she didn't need it, or she didn't need it at all and used it to solicit sympathy, which I would not have put past her.

She knocked long and loudly, several times, before opening the door with her key. We stepped inside, leaving the door open behind us.

The curtains, I could see, were drawn, both those in front and those that covered the patio door. With them closed, the room was fairly dim and full of shadows, but light enough to see that it was empty—completely empty—of everything that belonged to Shirley.

Ann reached for a switch near the door and turned on the ceiling light. There were empty spaces on the walls where Shirley's pictures had been, and a pile of what looked like Ann's needlework mottoes lay on the dinette table, as if she had intended to rehang them.

We moved to the back of the apartment and Ann opened the curtains there, allowing light in from outside. The sliding door to the patio was unlocked and open four or five inches, though the screen was shut.

The kitchen countertops were bare, as were the shelves in the cupboards over them.

Ann opened the refrigerator and found it and the freezer compartment similarly empty.

"She's moved out," Ann said. "But she'll probably come back for her security deposit."

"And the extra month's rent," I reminded her. But my thoughts were elsewhere.

Walking back into the living room, I paused beside the desk

in the alcove. It was bare of laptop computer, books, journal, notepad—everything. On the wall over it the small bulletin board remained, but it was empty of the calendar and list of phone numbers, which reminded me that I had copied that list and put it in the pocket of the skirt I had been wearing that day, where it probably still was.

My uneasy feeling was growing as we examined the place. How could Shirley have found another place to live between the time she vanished from my motor home and noon, when Ann said she had returned from the grocery and noticed that she was gone? Could she have moved out everything she owned in that short amount of time?

"Let's take a look at the bedroom and bath," I suggested, heading in that direction.

Off the living room there was a hallway with bedroom on one side, bathroom on the other, and a door at the end.

"Does that door lead into the garage?" I asked, half noticing that there was an odd hint of something slightly, unpleasantly metallic in the air, but focused on the door.

"Yes."

Passing the rooms to either side, I went directly along the hall and opened it.

A switch beside the door gave us light to see that a green sedan took up a large part of the space available in the small garage. Its doors and trunk were open and the interiors of both had been piled full of possessions that Shirley had moved out of the apartment. Everything was now in total confusion, tossed out onto the floor of the garage in a tangle of clothing, pots, pans, books, linens, costume jewelry, cosmetics, and other items. Suitcases had been emptied and thrown after their contents, boxes upended and pawed through, objects scattered without regard to their condition—a bottle of lotion had, for instance, broken upon hitting the cement floor and soaked what appeared to be a blue silk jacket. A small box lay next to what had been its contents—the things I had seen on Shirley's desk. But I noticed that neither the journal nor the laptop computer was there.

Still on the backseat of the car were her pictures, carefully cushioned with blankets and towels she had spread between them. I looked through them quickly and found that the abstract I had noticed on the living room wall was not among them—odd.

Moving out had obviously been her aim, but the open car doors and destruction of her possessions made it clear that she must have been interrupted—or gone mad—before completing the job.

Ann stood staring into the garage, her mouth open in surprise. "But . . ." She turned to me. "Where is she, then?"

Where indeed? I was now more than uneasy.

Going back along the hallway, I glanced hurriedly into the bedroom and saw only a pile of clothes on hangers that had been taken from the open closet and tossed haphazardly on a bed stripped of linen and pillows. Bedside tables stood with drawers gaping open and empty. A small suitcase had been emptied of lingerie by the door. Other than that the room was empty.

Swinging around, I crossed the hall and opened the bathroom door, heart in my throat, ignoring the hand Ann laid on my arm.

She was trying to say something, but I had no idea what, nor did I care. What did register was her gasp as she peered over my shoulder into the brightness from the one light in the place that had been left on.

"Oh," she said. *"Oh God!"*

Shirley's nude body lay supine, just beneath the surface in the tub full of crimson water, arms at her sides, legs straight, heels resting on either side of the faucet at the end of the tub as if, weakening from loss of the blood that had poured from the deep slashes on her arms, she had allowed herself to pass out and slip limply to her position under the water as she bled. Though her blood had made the water slightly opaque I could see that her eyes were open and staring. Her hair, now anything but blond, floated softly around her head. She was very clearly dead and had been in the water a long time.

Ann made a retching sound behind me.

"Don't throw up in here," I told her sharply. "Take it to the kitchen sink."

She disappeared abruptly, hand over her mouth.

I stepped in to take a closer look without touching anything and saw that the toilet seat was closed and a towel had been laid on it within reach of a bather. Strange for a suicide, which was what this appeared to be, to provide for drying herself later— habit, perhaps.

There was nothing else I could see that was out of place or that told a variant story. Only a medical examiner would be able to tell if she had died the way it appeared, but I noticed a mark on one of her ankles that looked as if it might have been a bruise.

I went back down the hall and into the living area of the place, expecting to find Ann, but it was empty. Across the living room was the door that I had assumed on my earlier visit was a closet. Now it stood wide open—revealing a passage between the two units of the duplex.

I remembered Shirley saying *I think she comes in sometimes when I'm not here.* So this was how Ann had gained access to Shirley's part of the building. She was an odd bird indeed.

Letting it go, I went through, found Ann's phone, and dialed 911. When the dispatcher answered, I asked for Herrera specifically and told her why.

"Is it a medical emergency?" she asked.

"Not now. The woman has clearly been dead for hours."

She told me they would send the necessary people immediately and that Herrera would be contacted as well.

I hung up the phone and sat down on one of Ann's doily-covered chairs to wait for the arrival of the police.

It wasn't until much later that I remembered I had intended to visit Alan Medina at his gallery and find out, if I could, why he had been following Shirley the day before in the plaza.

# Seventeen

There are sins of omission that we commit simply by not paying attention, or by shrugging off involvement. I had been relieved to have Shirley gone when she disappeared so abruptly the previous day, hadn't I? Though I think my reaction was somewhat defensible, I felt guilty about it nonetheless. It was one of those lemons life hands you, justifiable or not.

As we waited for Herrera, I wished that after my conversation with Shirley that evening in the motor home I hadn't suggested that we leave solutions to her problems until the next day. Tired as she had been, I might have learned something useful had we explored possibilities. I also remembered the niggling uneasiness I had felt about her story, which might have been resolved in further conversation. It was too late now. I would probably never know what it was that had bothered me.

Ann had splashed some water on her pale face and gone to lie down until we had help. She had said little, but muttered to herself as she left the room, "I should have known she'd show up. I shouldn't have . . ." The rest was unintelligible as she went through the door.

Glancing across the room, I noticed in particular one of her needlework mottoes on the opposite wall: THE ONLY EASY DAY WAS YESTERDAY. She'd certainly hit the mark with that one.

It must have been another slow day for Taos law enforcement, for it wasn't long until, with siren, a police car and a paramedic van pulled up in the street out front and the occupants came hurrying in. Clearly the dispatcher had not trusted my analysis of the condition of the deceased or, more probably, it was standard operating procedure.

Officer Herrera arrived shortly, after the paramedics had examined Shirley's body, declared her dead, and left the scene as it was for investigators and a medical examiner, necessary for a case of unattended death. A younger officer had talked first to Ann, recording what she could give him. She was so shaken that for once she seemed completely forthcoming, telling him what she had seen and heard of Shirley before going to the grocery the day before. She included the fact that we had gone looking for Shirley and why, referencing the previous carbon monoxide incident. He was just turning to me when Herrera showed up, took the report, and assumed responsibility for my interview.

"Could we go outside for this?" I asked him, feeling a need for air and to check on Stretch, who had now been in the car for well over an hour.

He agreed and we walked out in time to see that several neighbors were outside their houses, watching and wondering what was going on.

Stretch was fine, but I carried him with me and went with Herrera to sit in his patrol car with the windows down while I told him about coming to see Ann and finding Shirley's body. Stretch curled up in my lap, content to be held, and gave Herrera's hand a friendly lick when the officer reached to give his ears a rub.

"So the dead woman is the friend you said had stayed overnight with you night before last?" the officer asked and made a note when I nodded. "Tell me everything you can about her—and about finding her."

"Well, first, she was not a friend but an acquaintance," I began, and explained how I had met Shirley and why I had invited her to stay with me.

"So she tried to commit suicide two days ago?"

"That's the way it seemed, though she strongly denied it."

I went back to what Shirley had told me in the Winnebago—everything I knew about her divorce, her relationship with Anthony Cole, and the subsequent theft of her money.

"And she cleared out while you were away, leaving nothing to explain why? That's odd, isn't it?"

I agreed and told him about catching sight of her later in the plaza and the man who had been following her.

"Alan Medina? Interesting," he commented thoughtfully.

"Why?"

"He's on my radar—has a record," he said in answer to my questioning look.

There were a few moments of silence while he considered what I had told him, then glanced across at me, frowning.

"About this Anthony Cole person," he said. "You say he borrowed *a hundred thousand dollars* from her—cashed her check and disappeared? That's a lot of money for anyone to loan to someone she hadn't known long."

"She thought she knew him pretty well, I guess—they were evidently intimate. But that's just what she told me. From her story he seems to have been very slick about it and I'd guess it's probably not the first time."

"Can you describe him for me?"

I had to shake my head. "He was long gone before I even knew he existed. You should ask Ann Barnes—she met him more than once."

"I'll do that."

"The whole thing—her divorce and then the theft—may have been reasons she could have wanted to die."

He thought for a moment or two, once again frowning, then seemed to make a decision and looked up at me again.

"I'm considering that," he said slowly. "It *appears* that when her first attempt was interrupted by Mrs. Barnes, she stayed with you, then slipped out at the first opportunity and came back here to try again—and succeeded the second time. People often stick to their first choice of method in killing themselves, but maybe she didn't want the landlady to hear the car running and stop her again."

"But why would she pack up her things as if she was moving out, stop in the middle, trash it all, and slit her wrists?" I asked.

"That's an interesting question," he agreed. "And, just between you and me, there's another thing or two that make me wonder. There's a head injury—one of her pupils is blown. Either she fell in the tub—unlikely from the position of her body—or was hit with something. And there are a couple of bruises that make it look as if someone grabbed her hard by the ankles and yanked her under the water. We'll have to see if she has water in her lungs to tell if she drowned before she bled out."

"I noticed a mark on her ankle, but I assumed she probably lost consciousness and slid down under the water."

"She may have. But it's an unusual position—legs extended, feet on the far edge of the tub. I'd have expected her to have been sitting in the water and her knees to have bent as she slid down, which would have raised them above the water, but not her feet."

I was surprised that he was being so forthcoming about Shirley's death, but it soon became clearer when he paused for a moment, turned to face me directly, and asked the question he had been leading up to.

"Tell me, Ms. McNabb, what do you think of Ann Barnes?"

I knew what he was asking, but it didn't seem likely to me.

"She's the one who heard the car running and called for help night before last, when it would have been easy enough to leave it alone," I told him. "I think she's a lonely older woman, a confirmed busybody and a snoop—you noticed, I suppose, the door between the two units? But she lost her cookies when we found Shirley. I had to send her off to the kitchen or she would have added to the condition of the bathroom."

"Good thinking." Herrera grinned. "It wouldn't be the first time, but it's not something I'd encourage. On the other hand, I've known killers to have weak stomachs at their own handi-work."

An unmarked car drove up and parked, and a woman got out with a case in her hand.

"That's the ME," Herrera said. "Got to go. You're going to be around for a few days, right? I'll get back to you."

We both climbed out and he followed the woman up the walk to the duplex, giving me a wave before he disappeared.

I drove away feeling drained, a dozen questions competing for attention in my mind. I tend to hold on tight to my reactions in an emergency and to maintain a certain level of practicality when there is a need for it. You have to think straight in order to take care of what has to be done, whatever that is. But once again alone, in the wake of what had been a shock to my system, as it would be to almost anyone's, I felt cold and a little sick to my stomach. I couldn't blame Ann for throwing up. What we had discovered was anything but pleasant.

There was a deep sadness that I couldn't have prevented Shirley's death somehow. Had she killed herself? Or, as Herrera had intimated, could someone else have been responsible for her death? I felt again a sense of guilt at not wanting to be involved and realized that part of it was a natural reaction to the death of my friend Sarah, who had been murdered the previous fall. Following my suspicions and poking into the backgrounds of the people and circumstances that had surrounded her death had eventually created a threat to my life before the person responsible had been apprehended. I knew that the inclination to distance myself from this fatality was partly due to lingering reaction to that one. This was easier because Shirley had been a stranger, not a part of most of my life, as Sarah had been—close as a sister. Even so, if someone *had* murdered Shirley, there were enough similarities in the situations to make my hands leave clammy prints on the wheel of the car and my breathing a little more labored than normal.

I needed to step away from it, and I did. Instead of going, as I had planned, to see what I could learn from Alan Medina, I went straight home and took an extended shower, then had a nap—another way of coping with stress—and took a long, slow walk with Stretch.

It helped, but I could still feel the tension lying in wait for me in the form of questions. As we passed the campground office I caught the scent of honeysuckle from somewhere in the surrounding garden and thoughts of Sarah sprang immediately to mind because she had loved it so. Wondering if someone would have similar encounters with things associated with Shirley, I thought of her ex-husband. He would be the one likely to have comparable mentally recorded history—to be caught by the small, unexpected things and moments.

That brought to mind the numbers and e-mail addresses I had copied from the bulletin board above her desk. Could one of them belong to Ken as she had called him? Would Herrera make the same connection? Had she kept her married name, or taken back her maiden one? It was something Herrera would find out from going through her belongings for identification that would probably be found in her purse. Somewhere among her things should also be the list I had copied and her journal, which I had left unread. He should be alerted to look for them.

Back in the Winnebago, I went to the closet and found that list in the pocket of the skirt I had been wearing the day Pat and I had picked up Shirley at the hospital. Among the initials on it was a *K.M.*, with what appeared to be a phone number. *Ken Morgan?* Possibly—even probably, I thought, and was tempted to try it.

But what would I say if he answered in person? Notifying the man of the death of his ex-wife was not my responsibility; that should be done by someone in authority, not a passing acquaintance without the particulars of her demise. A postmortem would be required for this unattended death and it would be the better part of a week before the reports came in from the medical examiner in Albuquerque, where Herrera had told me all autopsies in the state were done, at the University of New Mexico School of Medicine's facility.

Instead, I put in a call to Herrera's office and left a message for him to call me when he had time. Then I turned my attention to getting ready for the evening with Butch at the opening reception at Weaving Southwest with dinner following.

Those plans brightened my mood considerably.

# EIGHTEEN

ON MY EXPLORATION OF THE TAOS PLAZA I HAD PICKED up a silky, rust-colored skirt that was gathered in horizontal bands and swung nicely a few inches from the floor. Alaskans dress quite casually for almost everything and I have never ascribed to the dress-for-success principle, so I seldom wear dressy skirts, feeling more comfortable in denim, or in slacks. But I decided to gussy up a bit for the reception, wear it with a black blouse and carry along the ruana I had knit of yarn from the shop in case the evening was cool.

I was adding my silver bracelets and earrings when Butch arrived to collect me. I was glad I had taken the trouble to dress, for he had abandoned his jeans and cowboy shirt in favor of slacks and a dress shirt open at the collar.

"You look very presentable," I told him.

"Well," he grinned, raising a pant leg enough to let me see that he still wore Western boots, though this pair was of beautifully tooled leather and had probably cost the moon. "You can take the boy out of the country, but—well, you know the rest.

I was born and raised just north of Missoula, Montana, so I hardly know how to walk in a pair of shoes. And so do you—look *very* presentable—by the way."

Leaving Stretch on guard duty, we took Butch's truck and arrived at Weaving Southwest at approximately seven thirty, to find a number of people there ahead of us. Some of them were friends and family of the weavers, but several appeared to be potential customers, and all were enjoying flutes of champagne as they strolled around admiring the rich colors and designs of the attractive rugs and tapestries displayed on the walls.

"Where's Stretch?" Pat inquired, after I had introduced her to Butch and he had wandered off to take a look around. "I thought you two were inseparably joined at the leash."

"He's pulling sentry duty at home to make sure no one breaks in again," I told her, forgetting that she didn't know about the previous night's incident.

*"You had a burglary?"*

I explained, then pulled her away to the back of the shop and briefly told her all that had happened in the last—could it possibly have been only twenty-four hours? I apologized for not calling her and explained that I felt it would be better to share it all in person. Hearing that Shirley was dead brought the expected surprise to her face, followed immediately by a frown of concern and regret.

"I can't believe it. How could she fool both of us so completely in denying that she had tried to kill herself?" she said. "Are they really sure she did it?"

I had to admit that it was possible it hadn't been suicide, but asked her not to say anything, especially to Connie, the gossip.

"If she doesn't already know, she soon will," Pat said in disgust. "She lies in wait for just such opportunities and will undoubtedly be showing up here. Just wait and see."

Sure enough—ten minutes after we had rejoined the rest of the crowd, Connie came hurrying in the door and made a bee-line for Pat. Before she could open her mouth, Pat took her firmly by the elbow and towed her off to the back, with me following in case she needed help, though I very much doubted she would.

"Don't even think about it," she told Connie sternly. "I already know about Shirley and I don't want a fuss made now, with a show in progress. Just keep it to yourself, or leave if you can't."

"But—but—" Connie sputtered.

"I *mean* it," Pat snapped, glowering. "This is neither the time nor the place."

"But she—"

"*There*," said Pat, pointing, "is the back door. *Use it!*"

Furious, Connie stomped out, giving us one black look before she disappeared.

"What was that all about?" Bettye Sullivan asked, coming up behind us and witnessing the dramatic exit.

"You really don't want to know," Pat told her, shaking her head as we moved back toward the center of the shop.

A young couple, clearly tourists who knew little about weaving and its tradition in the Southwest, came up with questions about one of the rugs that hung facing the front windows.

"We saw it from the street," the young woman said. "It was so gorgeous we had to come in and see it up close. How do you get such brilliant blues and reds?"

"Ask the expert," Pat told her, indicating Bettye, who was standing next to me. "Bettye dyes almost all our yarns, so she can tell you more than I ever could."

They moved across the room with her to take another look at the piece that had interested them, but Bettye turned back to me for a moment before following.

"You said you'd like to see the dyeing process. If you can come out tomorrow—I've decided to go ahead and do the reds."

"I'd love to. What time?"

"Ten or eleven in the morning will give me time to heat the water. Don't leave till I come back and draw you a map."

Butch had come ambling back to stand beside me and listened to this exchange.

"Come and see the rug I've fallen in lust with," he said, leading me off to see a medium-sized black, brown, and cream striped wool rug with a ruby red diamond pattern in the center that matched thin lines woven between the other three, alternating colors. It was a striking combination and I wasn't surprised when he turned to Pat with a grin.

"I'll take it," he told her. "I have just the place for it in my apartment in Santa Fe, but not on the floor. It'll go on the wall, just like this. Keep it away from the oil and grease I sometimes track in on my boots."

"Mechanic?" Pat asked.

"Trucker," he told her. "Well—ex-trucker, really. Accident on the Alaska Highway sort of changed my direction. That's where I met Maxie a while back."

In answer to Pat's questioning look, we explained how we met and the wreck of his truck. Back to business, he agreed to leave the rug on display for the time being, with a SOLD sign firmly attached.

"Or I could ship it down to you," Pat offered. "I appreciate your leaving it. It's nice to have the walls full for a few days after we've opened a new show."

"Not a problem," he told her. "But don't bother to ship it. I'll be back in two or three weeks for another evening of good food and music at the Taos Inn. I'll pick it up then, if that's okay."

"It'll be fine. Thanks."

She looked up from the sales slip she had been writing and waved as she called out, "Hey, Ford. I just sold your rug. Want to meet the new owner?"

I hadn't seen Ford Whitaker come in, but was pleased to introduce him to Butch and they seemed to hit it off. The two of them went back across the room—Ford answering questions about the materials and how the piece had been woven.

"Nice guy," Pat commented about Butch, when they were out of hearing distance.

I agreed—both were.

Bettye came back with the young couple she had been talking to and Pat had another sale to write up. While she did that, Bettye drew me a map of how to locate her adobe house on the mesa west of town.

"It's pretty easy to find. You'll know it's the right place when you see an old yellow pickup in front. It doesn't run anymore, I use it as a planter and fill the bed with flowers every year."

The map securely tucked away in my bag, I circled the shop, sipping champagne as I examined all the weavings on display. They made a colorful and interesting impression, many clearly influenced by the traditional southwestern patterns established by the Indians of the area. I was tempted by several, but considered the space available in the Winnebago and chose two colorful woven pillows instead.

Small profiles of the weavers were placed with their creations and I found it interesting that Alex George Sullivan, Bettye's husband, had a master's degree in art therapy and worked with emotionally disturbed adolescents in addition to his weaving and dyeing. Several others had come to weaving from backgrounds in other artistic techniques or schools. One was a retired airline pilot. Another had begun weaving in a Benedictine monastery, drawn to the rhythms of both monastic and artistic life, including the meditative, hypnotic quality of "the process of passing the shuttle through the warp and filling design areas with color."

There was much more to weaving than I would have anticipated. It made me eager to start my own process with Pat as a guide, though on a much smaller scale.

I was considering it when Butch arrived beside me.

"This is great," he said enthusiastically. "I've never paid much attention to weaving, but I'm going to now. From that small loom I noticed in your motor home, I'd guess you're about to try it out yourself."

I told him about my upcoming lessons scheduled for the next week. Then we crossed the room to say goodnight to Pat and headed out to dinner.

"Are you sure you don't mind eating somewhere other than the Taos Inn?" I teased him as we cruised south on Paseo del Pueblo.

"Not at all. I've been to Bravo before and like it a lot. You will too."

Settled at a table toward the back of the restaurant, I found the menu full of appealing suggestions, but finally settled on a shrimp fettuccine dish.

While we waited for our food, I told Butch about my

invitation to watch Bettye dye yarn the next day and asked if he would like to go along.

"Sure," he agreed. "It would be interesting to see how the yarn gets dyed all those great colors."

We decided on a time and I offered to give him lunch after driving out to the Sullivan house.

"Now," Butch said, leaning forward with both elbows on the table, "speaking of dyeing vats, what's this about a body being found in one this week? Someone was talking about it at the shop earlier."

I could have guessed that it would come up in conversation at the opening of the show, but with everything else that had gone on since I read about it in the paper I simply hadn't thought about it much. Remembering that I had folded the article after showing it to Pat and still had it in my bag, I took it out and handed it across the table.

Butch read it and looked up at me with a grimace.

"Can you imagine the shock of finding some dead guy in a boiling pot?" he asked. "If you'll excuse the observation, it gives a whole new meaning to the term dyeing—or dying, as the case may be."

What could I do but groan?

"Have you heard any more about it—who it was, who put it there?"

"The paper only comes out on Thursdays and I haven't heard any more—hadn't even thought about it. But I've been more than a bit distracted, with the break-in and then everything that went on this afternoon."

I told him all about going to see Ann, finding Shirley, and my subsequent conversation with Herrera.

"Good Lord—you've had quite a day," he said. "Do you think it's connected to the break-in—or to this guy in the vat, for that matter? Everyone involved seems to be associated with weaving in one way or another."

"Oh, I don't think so."

The idea of connections hadn't occurred to me. But why should it have? Weaving seemed only peripheral. But it was interesting that Butch had seen that kind of correlation in hearing about all that had happened in the last few days.

I carried the idea home with me in the back of my mind and—after we had found the rig un-intruded upon, Stretch eager for company, had coffee with Jameson, and Butch had driven off into the night—it surfaced again as I readied myself for bed.

Sometimes it's true that you simply can't see the forest for the trees. There *was* a connection through the weaving, which he had identified, but I couldn't see that it was anything but circumstantial. Was it? Shrugging it off, I went to sleep almost at once. I didn't wake until the sun was shining brightly on another beautiful day and I could hear a multitude of birds in the trees outside cheerfully greeting it.

# Nineteen

Driving out of town and up to the western mesa, we found the Sullivan house easily enough from the map Bettye had drawn for me the evening before and were soon pulling into a wide parking space in front. Off to one side I was delighted to see that she had meant what she said about the pickup, for there it sat, a faded yellow antique, minus tires, not yet full of the flowers she had mentioned, but I could imagine the colorful show they would make in such an amusing planter.

While I have no taste for cutesy decorating, I admire the humor in slightly twisted caricatures—recycling uses for things that they were never intended for in the first place. In general, I detest birdbaths that look like giant daisies, garishly colored plaster dwarves and cartoon characters, and plastic flamingos as yard decoration. But I have a friend who has created a covert "flamingo refuge" in the woods near her rural home. Friends and acquaintances send her the pink plastic critters they find in garage sales or secondhand stores—broken or whole, missing legs, necks taped to hold the heads on—whatever. Tongue firmly in cheek, she cares for them by putting them with others of their kind in a hilarious kindred grouping that staggers the imagination. Of this I wholeheartedly approve.

If I were asked to judge any contest of similar humorous bent, Bettye's pickup planter would have taken a blue ribbon.

She had evidently heard the tires-on-gravel sound of Butch's truck coming up the drive, for she stood waiting to meet us between the double doors of a gateway set into an adobe wall. She led us up a walk to the door of the attractive flat-roofed house of matching adobe through a front garden enclosed with a "coyote fence"—traditionally made of vertical aspen saplings or juniper branches held upright between posts. At several places along the edge the roof was indented with what Bettye called *canales,* meant to carry off melting snow or rainwater. She also told us that she and her husband had designed the house themselves and helped in the building of it, reminding me that many Alaskans do the same with logs as building material, making each cabin or house unique.

For some reason I had imagined that adobe houses would be dark inside, but the lovely room we stepped into quashed all such notions. Through large windows set deep in the thick earthen walls light streamed in to brighten the colors of tapestries, rugs, and pillows, along with pottery and other items of local artistry, bringing the room to vivid life. The ceiling reminded me of what I had seen at the Taos Inn—*latillas,* or peeled aspen saplings—laid close together and further reflecting the light from their pale surfaces.

Looking through the window in the eastern wall I could see the town of Taos in the distance, nestled against the foothills of the Sangre de Cristos.

"Must be a great view at night when you can see the lights in the distance."

"It is," Bettye agreed. "We planned it that way."

In another room full of natural light toward the back of the house sat her large loom, warped and ready for her to start a new tapestry. On shelves and in baskets on the floor were many kinds and colors of yarn in complementary and contrasting hues. It made me want to get started on a weaving of my own, though I knew I would never be dedicated enough to come anywhere near the expertise that was evident in her wonderful tapestries that I had seen at the shop and now saw on the walls of her house.

"Let's go out to the vats," she suggested, showing us through a back door. "The water should be just about the right temperature to add the dye."

As we left the house, I listened as Bettye answered several questions Butch put to her concerning the process and kinds of dye she used. He was more enthusiastic than I had thought he would be and I was glad I had taken him along to the show the night before. What a surprising interest for a former trucker to take in what is often thought of as a woman's art form. But, I remembered, Butch had been a pleasant surprise from the moment we met—in a coffee shop at Steamboat, just before the road plunged into a deep valley, as we headed north on the Alaska Highway. People are seldom what you stereotypically imagine they will be. Many of the "outlaws" that pass you on the highway riding Harleys are weekend warriors from business and industry off on jaunts, and the most sophisticated, moneyed men of professional repute can be the worst of bandits and thieves. That thought turned my mind to Anthony Cole and his theft of Shirley's money and trust while pretending to be a businessman of some standing.

We went around the end of another coyote fence by a storage shed and were suddenly standing next to two huge vats enclosed in insulating walls of rectangular concrete bricks. Steam was rising from one of them, evidently the one in which Bettye meant to dye the yarn.

Butch started to ask the question that had leaped to my mind as well.

"That dead man the other day? Was it . . ."

Bettye turned and gave him a straight look with a concerned expression on her face.

"Not in these vats," she told him.

"No—no. I mean *like* these."

"Well, yes—at least it was similar. Doris Matthews doesn't do commercial work, but she had one large vat that she used sometimes to dye large amounts of wool for the rugs she wove so it would all be exactly the same color."

I hurried to ask a question that would take us away from the uncomfortable subject. "Where does the yarn you dye come from, Bettye?"

"From a company back east that spins and prepares it for dyeing." She waved a hand at maybe a dozen fat hanks of yarn, each with its own separating cord. They hung all together from a huge hook that would allow them to be lowered into the water of the vat.

"That's wool, isn't it? I always thought wool would shrink if you put it in hot water."

She smiled. "A lot of people think that, but it's really agitation that felts wool. Besides, the water is heated first and the fire put out before I add the dye, then the wool."

Butch had hunkered down to look under the vat to where the remains of a fire were still smoking slightly.

"You use wood?" he asked.

"Cheaper than the electricity or gas it would take to heat fifty gallons of water," she told him. "Especially since we have a couple of contractors who know we'll be glad to come and collect the scrap from their building projects if they give us a call. I seldom have to buy wood. Someone cuts down a tree? I'm very handy with a chain saw."

Butch was still checking out the vats, but I watched, fascinated, as Bettye stepped into the storage shed, put on a respirator mask and rubber gloves, checked a recipe from a notebook, and carefully measured out powdered red dye from gallon-sized cans into a container on a triple-beam balance scale that measured its weight in grams.

"Must be a job changing the water in those vats," he said, coming up behind me to see what was going on.

"In desert country we try to conserve as much as possible, so I only change it a few times a year," she told him. "That's part of why I measure so carefully. By the time the yarn is the color I want, it will have soaked up every bit of the dye I put into the water and left it clear."

With a huge paddle, she stirred the dye into the hot water in the vat, then lowered the white yarn into the crimson brew.

"Now it just takes time," she said. "I'll come out and move it around with the paddle a little once in a while until it's done, pull it out, let it drip, and hang it to dry. Come, I'll show you some I dyed yesterday."

We left the vats and walked back toward the house, where I noticed that Bettye had hung yarn to dry on long poles balanced between the top of a fence and one high step of a ladder.

In the noon sun it all but glowed in bright shades of blue and green. Lovely.

We thanked her for showing us the process and were soon back on the road to Taos and the RV park. There we found Stretch, full of delight in seeing Butch, who took him for a walk while I made a quick lunch for him to take along on his drive back to Santa Fe, since he had decided it was time to hit the road.

As I was filling his thermos with iced tea the pair of them came back, Butch with a thoughtful expression on his face.

"I can't imagine why anyone would want to put a body in a vat like that," he said, shaking his head. "It would obviously be found and identified, so they must not have cared about that. It was either intentional or they had no choice. Could it have been done to throw suspicion on the woman who owned the vat? Have you thought any more about connections with the rest that's been going on?"

I told him I had no ideas, except that it all seemed to have a common thread through weaving, though I couldn't see how.

"But I don't know any of these people well," I said thoughtfully. "And there are some that I don't know at all that I suppose could be connected peripherally."

I had—I thought, but didn't mention—one stone left that I wanted to turn. I had yet to meet or speak with Alan Medina and that was definitely on my afternoon agenda.

"Well," said Butch, "I'd better get going. I'm going to take the longer, historic High Road this time. Keep meaning to do it and haven't yet. It'll take more time, but it's supposed to be interesting—the road the original settlers took to get here."

"Will you be back soon?"

"Not next weekend. I'm going to make a run to Phoenix, but I could come up the following weekend. Will you still be here in two weeks?"

"I'm not sure. I may be, but it depends on how my weaving classes go and—oh, I don't know. Why don't you give me a call? Wherever I am you can reach me on my cell phone."

We exchanged numbers and addresses, both pleased that we would be able to keep in touch now that we'd found each other again.

"Give my address and phone to Jessie when you have a chance," he said, looking up the steps at me as he left. "I'd like to see her again sometime and meet that trooper friend of hers. Give her my best."

I promised I would.

"And you." He grinned. "You take good care—kiting around the country seems to get you involved in all kinds of things. Be careful, okay? Someone could take an interest the wrong way, you know?"

"At least it's never boring—but I will."

As Stretch and I watched him go, waving as he turned the corner and drove out of sight down the road, I was glad to have met him again and knew I'd miss him. It seemed much quieter than it had been for the last couple of days. As the dust settled behind his pickup, I went inside and sat down with a glass of iced tea of my own to think out some kind of plan for the afternoon.

The huge Class A Fleetwood had left sometime while we were visiting Bettye Sullivan and apart from a pop-up rig and a couple of tent campers the park was now empty. It was warm, dry, and, except for the faraway hum of traffic on Paseo del

Pueblo Sur, sleepily silent enough to tempt me toward a nap. Through the open window, I heard the zip of a grasshopper's wings as it flew somewhere in the nearby brush.

But I wanted to track down Medina and get that off my mental plate, so I finished my drink and got ready for another trip to downtown Taos.

# TWENTY

I WORE A BROAD-BRIMMED STRAW HAT AND MY SUNGLASSES, for the sun was bright and warmer than it had been since I arrived. It wouldn't be long, I thought, until I should think about hitting the road for somewhere that would be cooler. Even Taos, in its high and mountainous location, would have average temperatures in the upper eighties before long. But almost everywhere in the interior of the Lower Forty-eight is warmer in the summer than I am used to on the coast of Alaska, where the average high temperatures from June to August are between sixty and seventy degrees.

Once again leaving Stretch at home, I drove to the Taos Plaza and parked the car. From there I walked east across Paseo del Pueblo and along the left side of Kit Carson Road, where almost immediately I came to the Kit Carson Museum, which I had read contained a part of what had been the Carson residence, purchased by Carson as a wedding present for his bride, Maria Josefa Jaramillo, and was now a museum dedicated to him as one of America's great frontiersmen.

*Later,* I thought, passing it by. There would be plenty of time in the next week or two for museum inspections. I had another goal in mind for that afternoon.

Not far up the street, among other galleries and gift shops, I came to the Medina Gallery, a fairly small place with a display of unusual pottery in the front window, which gave me an excuse to go in and ask touristy questions.

At first the place seemed empty of anything but high-end art—mostly sculpture, pottery, and paintings tastefully exhibited. Classical music played quietly in the background. As I stood examining one of the pots I had selected among those in the window, a well-dressed Hispanic woman came out of a room at the back.

"May I help you with something?" she asked with a smile.

"This is interesting." I showed her the piece I was holding— a small, round pot that could be held in your cupped hands, its sides cut into steps that narrowed as they rose. An attractive pinkish tan in color, its surface glittered with thousands of tiny bits of gold. "Was it made locally? What kind of glaze did the potter use?"

"No glaze at all," she said. "The finish on micaceous pottery is a natural result of mica in the clay. All the pieces we have were made by a local potter at the pueblo just outside of town."

"It's beautiful. I've never seen anything like it."

Intending to attempt to contact Alan Medina, I found I had fallen in love with the piece. I buy very little in my travels, having collected a fair amount of Alaskan art over the years, which pretty much fills my house in Homer. But once in a long while I find something I simply can't resist. This was clearly one of those times, so without even looking at the other pots I handed her my credit card and asked her to pack it for shipping.

Besides, it provided me with a legitimate reason to remain in the gallery.

As we walked to the counter in the back I gave myself a mental shake to return my thoughts to my initial objective.

"Does Alan Medina work here?" I asked.

She nodded, focused on writing up the sale. "Yes, he does, but not today. He'll be back on Monday. Was there something . . . ?" She allowed the sentence to trail off unfinished and gave me a questioning look.

"Nothing that won't wait, I guess."

I thought quickly, hoping to gain some kind of information. She did look young, but not *that* young. However, nothing ventured in flattery, nothing gained. "You must be—his sister?"

She gave me a knowing and amused smile as she shook her head and corrected me, as I had known she would. "I'm Dolores Medina—his mother. Was it something *I* could help you with?"

Another bit of quick thinking required.

"A friend recommended Alan and the gallery to me because I admired a painting she had on her wall. If he'll be here Monday I could stop in again. But thank you anyway."

"We offer the work of a number of artists. Do you know the name?"

"Sorry, I don't."

"Well, you're welcome to look around. You may recognize the artist's style. Let me know if I can help."

I thanked her and spent a few minutes walking around the gallery. The art on its walls was attractive, carefully selected and displayed—and expensive. On one wall were displayed two handwoven rugs, in traditional colors and patterns that reminded me of the one Butch had bought the evening before. A bronze sculpture of a bird in flight stood on a pedestal next to them. There was more pottery filling one corner, with traditional painted Indian patterns in attractive contrasts of white, black, red, and tan.

Halfway around the room I was stopped cold in surprise. Hanging on the east wall was the colorful abstract acrylic I had seen in Shirley's apartment. For a moment or two I assumed it was only similar, for how could it be there for sale? But in stepping near to examine it more carefully I knew immediately and without a doubt that it was the same painting. There was another possibility: I had not looked closely at the one in the duplex. Could Shirley's picture have been a copy? I didn't think so—and it *had* been missing from the others she had put in the backseat of the car she had been packing, but—

Turning to Dolores Medina, who was working with something at the counter, I asked, "Do you have prints of any of the pictures?"

"Oh, no," she said. "We sell only originals and on an exclusive agreement with the artists."

Well, that answered that. I asked no further questions, thanked the woman who had sold me the pot, which, now carefully packed in a box, I took with me, and started toward the front of the gallery.

As I reached for the handle I heard a door slam in the back of the place and turned to see who had come in. Mrs. Medina was just disappearing behind a curtain that swung between the display area and what was apparently the storage and working part of the gallery. I was just able to hear a quick, low mumble of conversation with one sharply spoken word I couldn't catch, then the sound of the back door closing again. Whoever had come in had gone back out in a rush. I wondered if it could have been Alan, but we had never met, so why would he have avoided me? He wouldn't even know who I was or what I looked like, would he? I decided my imagination must be working overtime and went out the door onto the street.

Walking toward the plaza, where I had parked, I came to the corner and glanced left to check for oncoming traffic before stepping off the curb. When I looked right for the same reason, among the people ambling along in the Saturday afternoon sunshine one figure stood out—a man taking long, hurried strides past the Taos Inn. Alan Medina, I was almost sure, though I couldn't see his face to be certain it was the man I had seen on Thursday following Shirley in the plaza. Stepping back into a handy doorway, I watched him cross the street at a trot, reach Bent Street, and start to make a quick left. As he turned the corner, he glanced back over one shoulder, making me glad I had anticipated the move, for it was surely Medina.

Why would he run from me? It didn't make sense. I stood staring after him, confused. But it was obvious that I wasn't going to see or talk with him before Monday, if then. What the heck was going on? Did it have something to do with the reason Shirley's painting was now in the Medina Gallery, as I believed it must?

Whatever the answer was, I saw no way to solve the puzzle at the moment, so I went back to my car and drove home, where I picked up Stretch and took him along on a drive I had found on a map, the Enchanted Circle. I was up for any enchantment I could get after the past days of confusing and unpleasant events.

Hoping the escape would clear my head, I drove out of town past the Taos Pueblo, where my micaceous pot had been made, into the lush green of the Hondo Valley to the north. I took my time driving the eighty miles, stopping infrequently along the road that circled Wheeler Peak, New Mexico's highest, at 13,161 feet. Along the way was a variety of interesting things, but as my goal was simply to leave behind the confusion of busy streets and the happenings of the past few days, I passed most of them, including the D. H. Lawrence Memorial, where the author's ashes had been placed in a chapel built by his wife on the ranch where he had spent time writing in the 1920s. Some say that she mixed his ashes in the concrete used to make the altar inside the small white building I had seen in a brochure.

Beyond a huge scar left by a forest fire on the mountains, and a fish hatchery, we reached the small town of Questa. There I took the time to visit Artesanos de Questa, a cooperative showcase for local woodworkers, tinsmiths, painters, stained-glass artists, and sculptors, but did not add to my personal collections, though their work was appealing and diverse.

After a steep climb to the east with wonderful views of dark spruce and aspen still in its bright spring green on the slopes of the hills around Mount Wheeler, Red River was our next stop. We walked a bit through what was one of the numerous winter skiing resorts, but a pleasant place in any season with an Old West feel to its saloons and shop fronts—even a melodrama theater.

Cruising over Bobcat Pass, past the turnoff to the old gold-mining community of Elizabethtown, the beautiful Vietnam Veterans Memorial on a hill, and two more ski areas, I took us into Taos Canyon, heading west on the last part of the circle.

After a few miles on the road that twisted like a ribbon, we came to a roadside parking area where I pulled over and we found a place to sit in the shade of ponderosa pines and appreciate the spectacular cliffs of the Palisades Sill across the Cimarron River that long before had carved its way down through igneous rock. It was cool and pleasant, with the music of the river for company as it gurgled along on its tumultuous way to join the Rio Grande for the cross-country run to the Gulf of Mexico. It was good to be away from people for the time being and I refused to consider any of the unsettling events of the past week in favor of letting nature soak in.

A crow swept down, hoping for a handout, and landed fairly close to where we sat. Stretch, always ready to defend against intruders, especially when they are even slightly smaller, dashed to the end of his leash and told it to get lost with yaps from as close as he could get. It was clear that the bird had calculated the limit of his mobility exactly, for it stayed just far enough out of reach to frustrate and annoy, cockily walking back and forth, watching his reaction with seeming amusement in its bright, intelligent eyes.

"Come here, you silly galah," I told him, tugging on the leash. "You can't win, you know. It's got your number."

He came reluctantly back and lay down beside the rock on which I was sitting, looked up at me with resignation in those irresistible brown eyes, and laid his muzzle down on his front paws.

Refusing to be further baited, he didn't even look around when the crow took off for parts unknown.

I gave him an approving pat. "You're right. Ignoring it is much the best policy."

I do so love Daniel's dog. He is such good company and never, never boring. What would I do without him?

By just after five o'clock we were back in Taos and settled in
the Winnebago. I opened all the windows to let out the warm,
stale air, then closed them again before turning on the air conditioner, pouring myself a glass of tea, and waiting for it to
grow cooler. It had been so warm that I didn't want to cook
anything and add to the heat, so I decided I would go back to
Bravo for dinner in an hour or so.

A note had been waiting for me on the door when I unlocked it:

> *2:45 p.m. Got your message. Will stop again later today*
> *or tomorrow morning.*
>
> *Herrera*

Sorry to have missed him, I had to think for a minute just
what it was I had been going to tell him. Oh, yes—that I might
have the phone number of Shirley's ex-husband, Ken Morgan,
on the list I had copied from her bulletin board and that he
might be able to answer questions about her—at the very least,
he should be told she was dead. Also, now, I supposed I should
tell Herrera about finding her painting in the Medina Gallery
earlier that afternoon.

That started the whole puzzle whirling in my thoughts
again, which I stubbornly refused to allow. Retrieving the
mystery I had picked up at Moby Dickens, I settled at the
dinette table and took myself off to North Carolina with *Rituals of the Season*. Stretch, after lapping up half a bowl of water, came and curled up beside me for a nap with his head on
my knee.

"You're such a bonzer boy, you are," I told him with appreciation.

At six thirty I left him and drove to Bravo, where I spent over an hour enjoying a Caesar salad with grilled chicken, prepared by someone else and therefore not heating up my living space.

Satisfied and tired, I headed home, parked the car next to the Winnebago, and walked around to find the coach door standing wide open, screen and all. The single light I had left on for Stretch showed me that there had been no more destruction that another burglary would have caused, but obviously someone had been in my rig again.

Cautiously stepping inside, I immediately spotted a note placed strategically on the dinette table—block letters, all capitals. My heart fell straight into my shoes as I read:

WE HAVE YOUR WEENER DOG. GIVE US WHAT
SHIRLEY MORGAN LEFT WITH YOU OR HE DIES.
IF YOU WANT HIM BACK PUT SOMETHING RED
IN THE WINDOW AND WAIT FOR A CALL.

# TWENTY-ONE

EVERYTHING GREW A LITTLE DARK AROUND THE EDGES and I had trouble catching my breath. A great pain of anguish grew in the center of my chest as I stood there with the note in my hand, staring at the words that seemed to swim on the page. Then I dropped it, whirled, and went from one end of the Winnebago to the other, calling for him and looking—sure that it couldn't be true and that he must be there somewhere.

Of course he wasn't—not anywhere. I even looked in all the cabinets and closets, went outside and opened every storage space under the motor home.

All sorts of thoughts went through my mind: If I had only taken him with me and left him in the car at the restaurant—if I had made dinner for myself at home and not gone out at all—if I had never taken to the road like a gypsy and stayed in Alaska where I belonged. I wished that Butch Stringer had not gone back to Santa Fe. It was desperation and I knew it—and that I was being totally irrational. But it was like having one of my children snatched.

I dearly love that dog.

And Daniel had entrusted him to *me*.

*Oh, Daniel, I'm sorry. It's all my fault and I'm so very, very sorry.*

There wasn't room in my head for what Daniel might have said in reply—probably several Aussie curses at the circumstances.

It was only when I slowly began to settle down that I thought to call the police.

Herrera arrived in less than fifteen minutes. By the time he got there I had shed a few tears—and I almost never cry. But they were angry tears, and that reaction was growing. Life on the Last Frontier doesn't create many wimps. We Alaskans don't take threats lightly, or knuckle under. We tend to get involved. In times of trouble we take care of each other and I meant somehow to take care of Stretch as I had promised Daniel I would.

I unlocked the door, let Herrera in, and handed him the note without a word. He read it, glanced up in a concerned assessment that told him how angry and determined I was.

"Well," he said, "this certainly changes the equation. Have you got a cup of coffee?"

*"Coffee?"*

"I'd say we'd better talk and it may take a while. But I need to get the guys working on anything they can find here."

I didn't think I needed the caffeine, but made a pot anyway while he called back the investigation crew, who dusted black fingerprint powder over my living space again, mostly around the dinette and on the door I had found open. When they had finished and gone, I cleaned it off and poured us coffee before sitting down across from him at the table.

Interrupting only once or twice, he sipped at his coffee and took rapid and copious notes as I told him everything I could think of that had happened, or that I had learned since I arrived in Taos, or that I thought could possibly relate to the reason for Stretch's abduction. I included the phone number that might be for Shirley's ex-husband, Ken Morgan, also that I had found her abstract painting on the wall of the gallery and spotted Alan Medina hurrying away on the street outside. It all seemed impossibly related, yet unconnected at the same time, and I could only hope that he could make better sense of it than I could.

"What do they want?" he asked, when I finally wound down. "What did Shirley Morgan leave with you?"

"*Nothing!* She left nothing. I have no idea what they want."

Not knowing what they wanted was a large part of what was making me anxious and angry.

"Whatever it is they think I have, it's probably what they tore the place apart looking for on Thursday and may have torn Shirley's things apart looking for on Friday."

"You're right. And if this is an indication, they clearly didn't find it." He held up the note. "Well, at least we know from this that there's more than one of them. Interesting."

"There may be. But what are we going to do?"

He looked at me with narrowed eyes and shook his head.

"*You,*" he said, suddenly all law enforcement official, "are going to do *nothing*. You will stay here and do exactly what they say to do—hang something red in the window and wait to see if you can find out what they want."

*Stay there?* I may have been angry and ready to help in getting Stretch back, but I'm no dummy either. A woman of my age is no match physically for someone like Alan Medina and whoever else might be involved—and I had decided he had to be part of the thing. I told Herrera that I didn't like the idea of being alone if they—whoever *they* were—came back.

"You won't be. There've been two murders in the last week and I'm not interested in having another. So I've put someone outside to watch this place. You won't see him and neither will they, if they come back, but he's already there—armed—if you need him."

*Armed?*

I hesitated for a long minute, thinking hard about my shotgun in the concealed space in the Winnebago, before I asked with cautious phrasing, "Would it be wise if I were armed as well?"

There was a longer pause as he gave me a sharp, perceptive look, then said, choosing his own words carefully, "A license or permit to possess a rifle, shotgun, or handgun is not required in New Mexico. Interstate transportation is another thing and the carrying of a concealed weapon is forbidden. Would you know how to use . . . such a firearm . . . *if* you had one?"

"I grew up using rifles and shotguns."

"Ah-h." He nodded and added a caution to our carefully hypothetical topic of conversation. "Firearms can be turned on their owners, you know."

I nodded.

We understood each other.

After giving me a number with which to reach him directly, which I programmed into my cell phone as a one-touch number, he was soon gone.

I stood at the door, looking out into the brush and trees that surrounded the RV park next to where I was parked, and wondered just where my guardian angel was hidden. The only nearby sound was a cricket chirping in the dark, so wherever he was he was keeping very still. A light breeze rustled the leaves and swept the scent of sage into my face. I took a deep breath, closed and locked the door, then took a red blouse from the closet—that *something red* to hang as a signal.

*Oh, lovie, where are you?* I thought, as I secured it in the window over the table, hoping against hope that *they* were treating Stretch well.

Can you call it kidnapping when the victim is a dog?

It was one of the worst nights I have spent in my life.

I had handed over responsibility for Stretch's welfare to someone else and it was both a relief and a frustration to have done so. That Herrera would do his best I had no doubt. He was a kind man and seemed not just good at his job but resourceful and respectful of the people involved as well. But would he care enough about an animal? I thought he would, for as he left, standing below the coach steps, he had turned to look up at me.

"I have a Yorkshire terrier," he said. "Puñado rides with me sometimes. We'll do our best to find your dachshund, Ms. McNabb."

Find him? I would rather he had said "rescue him," but I knew what he meant and would take what I could get in terms of language.

As soon as he was gone I got out the shotgun, made sure it was loaded and ready to fire, and propped it against the wall next to my bed. Then I lay down without undressing and tried, unsuccessfully, to rest.

There was little sleeping, or even snoozing lightly. The breeze would periodically rattle something outside and bring me fully awake again and sitting up in the bed. After midnight, when it died, a couple of coyotes howled a duet for half an hour, reminding me of how they had sung on the night Shirley had stayed over.

Poor Shirley. Herrera had said little about her death in answer to my questions, just that they now knew for sure that it had been a homicide and that the investigation was ongoing. But his attention and focus on the current developments told me that for his own reasons he felt there was a serious connection.

I thought that was pretty obvious, and shoved the pieces to the puzzle of the last few days around and around in my head, but they seemed to have been mixed together from more than one box, for I couldn't make several of them fit at all—the dead man in the dye vat, for instance, and Shirley's painting.

Why did the people who had taken Stretch think she had left something with me? One or more of them must have all but torn apart the Winnebago in their hunt for it. It was clear that both their intensive exploration and the theft of Stretch were related to getting what they wanted, whatever it was. In their search they had not found the secret hidey-hole where my shotgun usually resided. Could there be other places they had missed—that *I* had missed? Possibly. That would depend on the size and shape of the item, wouldn't it? Anything of a noticeable size would have been quickly found. So it had to be something small, or the right shape to have been slipped in, under, or behind something else.

The idea took me back to my friend Sarah's death and a number of hiding places in her Victorian house that had figured largely in revealing her murderer. We had amused ourselves with secret spaces as roommates in college and the habit endured through the years. But we had learned a lot about how to hide things in ordinary places. Could I use what I had learned back then to find something I only suspected that Shirley had left in the Winnebago?

Swinging my feet out of bed and turning on lights as I went from one end to the other of the motor home, I searched for over an hour and came up empty and frustrated. There was always the possibility that I was hunting for something that wasn't there at all, but somehow I didn't think so. It made such good sense that she might have left it where she hoped they wouldn't think to look. Someone must have been following her that night to know she had stayed with me.

At four o'clock I gave up and turned out the lights again before returning to the bed. It seemed so strange to be there by myself, with no small friend in the basket beside me or curled up behind my knees under part of a quilt or bedspread. It was quiet—so quiet. I missed hearing him breathe and roll over periodically. I missed . . .

It was a soft knock at the coach door that woke me to another bright and sunny morning. The clock read seven o'clock—I had slept for almost three hours.

"Who is it?" I called through the door.

"Officer Jim Tolliver, Ms. McNabb. Wanted you to know I'm going off duty now. Call if you need us."

I opened the door to find a tall young man looking up at me with a high-powered rifle in one hand, nightscope and all. He looked tired and dusty from lying all night on the ground somewhere in the brush.

"My guardian angel."

He grinned, saluted, and was gone.

*Blessings on him,* I thought, *and on the head of Officer Herrera.*

Locking the door again, I went to take a shower while the coffee brewed, leaving the cell phone within reach so I could hear it if it rang.

It didn't.

# Twenty-two

THE FIRST COUPLE OF HOURS OF THAT MORNING PASSED so slowly that I felt if the clock had been an hourglass I would have been able to watch one grain of sand fall at a time. Half the time I sat staring out the window, watching clouds float overhead that for the first time looked a little gray, as if they might hold rain, and half of it I paced back and forth between the front and back of the Winnebago.

The phone remained ominously silent. I didn't know how they could have the number of my cell phone, but it was the only phone I had, so they must have obtained it somehow. All I could do was wait, as directed.

Coming back past the galley after one such circuit, without thinking I reached under the sink for the kibble to fill Stretch's empty bowl. With it in my hand I realized what I was doing and the whole loss of him that I had been keeping at bay with anger swept over me again. Unable to see for the tears that welled up along with a surge of hot fury, I blindly tossed the bag back into the compartment and kicked the door shut so hard I thought I had broken a toe. Limping across to the sofa to sit down and find out, I soon knew it wasn't broken, but the pain provided an excuse for my red eyes and damp face when I answered Herrera's knock at the door.

He stepped in and noticed my limp.

"What did you do?" he asked.

"Something stupid," I told him. "Never mind. It's not critical."

I waved him to the table and poured us both coffee.

"My officer says there was no sign of anyone but that you were up most of last night."

"I was trying to find what they seem to think she left with me and want back," I admitted. "I couldn't find a thing, but then I have no idea what I'm looking for, so it's hard to know where to look. Anyway, it may not be here at all."

"Maybe we can find out more when they call. I've got someone listening, so it's worth a try if you can keep them talking as long as possible. For now, there's something else you may find interesting. You already know about the body found in the weaver's dye vat last Tuesday."

"It was in Thursday's paper."

"Yes, well. It turns out he was not a local, but a man with a considerable record up and down the western half of the country. His real name is Earl Jones, but he's had several aliases, one of them Tony Jones, and"—he looked up and grinned—"wait for it—*Andrew Coleman.*"

Andrew Coleman—Anthony Cole. They were too close for coincidence. "So you think—"

"Yes, we think he was the Anthony—'Tony'—Cole that Shirley told you had conned her out of that big check."

A previously unconnected piece of my mental puzzle slid neatly into place. But how had he ended up in the vat and who had—?

"But she said he had left town."

"Maybe she just assumed he had and he was lying low—or he came back for some reason. Anyway, he had to be here to get himself killed, didn't he? And it gives *her* a hundred-thousand-dollar motive."

True.

"I know you never saw him, but do you know of anyone who could positively identify him?"

I thought back to the day I had first met Shirley and taken her home from the hospital—the day I had heard her story about Tony. I couldn't remember if Pat had said she ever met him, but Ford Whitaker had at least seen him with Shirley.

"And Ann Barnes," I told Herrera. "She evidently liked him enough not to mind his moving into the duplex."

"Good," he said. "I'm going to go find these folks and see if they can identify him from a photo or two we have from his record of arrests. I'll be back, but I'll be told if they call you. Don't leave here without letting me know, right?"

"Right."

But Herrera was no more than ten minutes gone when there was not the sound of my cell phone but a knock on my door.

I opened it and found the manager of the park outside.

"You have a phone call at the office," she told me. "We don't usually take personal calls, but he said it was long distance and an emergency. Will you come?"

"Of course," I told her, my thoughts immediately turning, of course, to the welfare of my children. But realizing that I might miss the call I was waiting for on the cell phone, I snatched it up along with my bag and keys, locked the door, and hurried with her to the office. Halfway there it occurred to me that Joe and Carol usually called me on the cell phone and an ominous feeling that the caller would be neither of them grew. I would have to call Herrera and let him know.

"Hello," I said into the office phone.

"So you *have* got what we want," an unidentifiable whisper rasped in my ear. "Still want your mutt?"

What could I do? If I said *no,* it would probably be saying *yes* to Stretch's death.

"Yes," I told him—at least I thought it was a him.

"Good. Smart lady. Now here's the deal. You will *not* contact that cop that's been hanging around. We'll know if you do."

So they had been watching.

"Or the one who spent the night outside."

Watching closely.

"Now listen up. Wrap the thing in something waterproof, take it with you, and drive to the Taos Plaza. Park in the first place you come to and walk to Charley's Corner at the north end. Go through the store and into the stockroom, then out the back door, where you'll find a Dumpster. Toss the package into the Dumpster and go back inside and shut the door. Walk back to your car and drive around to where you left the package. If you've given us what we want, you'll find your mutt in the Dumpster. If you haven't . . ." His voice trailed off threateningly. "You've got half an hour, so you better hurry. Got that?"

I swallowed hard.

"You got that?" he demanded.

"Yes," I managed to croak out, trying to think. "But I don't . . ."

There was a click and I was alone on the line.

I laid the receiver back in the cradle and turned to find the manager standing close behind me.

"Bad news?" she asked. "Are you okay?"

"I don't know," I told her truthfully, heading quickly for the door. "But I've got just half an hour and am going to the plaza. If *anyone* asks, please tell them that, will you?"

I couldn't wait for her answer.


Halfway into downtown Taos it crossed my mind to wonder why, with all the police presence in the last day or two, she hadn't come around to find out what was going on in her RV park. Would Herrera think to ask her if she'd seen me leave? I hoped so, though she wouldn't be able tell him anything but where I was going. Glancing behind me on the road, I could see no police car, or anyone who seemed to be following me, as I both hoped and dreaded there might be. I was on my own.

As usual, where Paseo del Pueblo narrowed as it came into downtown the traffic was heavy, even for a Sunday. Bumper to bumper it crawled along, making me crazy with frustration. Then, at the turnoff for the plaza I had to wait for the light to turn yellow in order to make a quick left turn and my watch told me I had just over five minutes left. Finding a space halfway along, I parked in front of the New Directions Gallery, tumbled out, and walked, as I had been told, to Charley's Corner, though I have never walked so fast in my life. Inside, I headed straight through to the back, only to be hailed by a clerk near the stock-room door. Why can you never find one when you need one, but they're all over you when you don't? Ignoring her, I pushed my way past and into the back, hearing her behind me.

"Stop. Customers are not allowed in there."

"It's an emergency," I tossed back over a shoulder and kept going.

"I'm getting the manager," she threatened.

"Please do."

By the time she brought a manager—if, indeed, there was one working on a Sunday—I would have accomplished my immediate goal. Though what the kidnappers would do when they found not what they wanted—whatever that was—but Margaret Maron's latest mystery, *Rituals of the Season*—which, damn and blast, I hadn't even finished reading yet—I had no idea. I could only hope that in their hurry to collect the package I had prepared by wrapping it in newspaper and tying it securely in not one but three plastic grocery bags they would simply snatch it, toss Stretch into the Dumpster, and take off, fearing recognition or, worse, that I had unknowingly been followed. I was both fearful, and hopeful, of that myself.

Outside the back door, adrenaline at an all-time high, I glanced around. Still it seemed that I was by myself. The Dumpster stood handily next to the door, too tall to see inside. So I set down my bag and the package with the book, took a step and jumped high enough to firmly grasp the top and pull myself up to peer into it, hoping for Stretch, but I saw only that it must have been recently emptied, for just a small amount of trash barely littered the bottom. In case there was anyone watching, I then lowered myself back down and made a display of tossing the package into the bin. I heard a thump as it hit the side and a crunch as it rebounded onto a pile of shredded packing paper I had seen below.

Turning slowly, I took a good long look around to see if I could spot anyone watching, but there was only a couple in the crosswalk headed for the plaza and a man who pulled his car into a space in the lot opposite, got out, locked the door, and walked away without so much as a glance in my direction. It was time to follow instructions and leave.

The first thing to get in the way of doing that occurred when I tried to open the door to go back into Charley's shop and found it had locked behind me. Rattling the handle and pounding on it did no good in terms of response, so I gave up and trotted around the corner and along the side street into the plaza. The second thing came when I dashed the half block to my rental car and arrived just in time to see Herrera pull his squad car up behind it, effectively blocking my exit from the parking space.

Frustration growing, I gestured wildly for him to drive forward, but instead he opened the door and got out.

"Ms. McNabb?" he asked, walking toward me. "It's not smart for you to be down here by yourself instead of—"

"Please move out of the way," I interrupted, afraid that if whoever had Stretch opened the package and found it did not contain what they had demanded, they might take out their anger on him. "I've *got* to get out of here—*right now!*"

"—letting us take care of this," he finished, reaching me as I unlocked the car and opened the door to get in.

"Look," I told him, sliding behind the wheel, starting the engine, and jamming the gearshift into reverse. "I'm following timed instructions and you're about to lose my dog for me—probably get him killed. I haven't time to argue, so move and let me out of here."

Frowning, he still hesitated.

"On one condition," he said.

"What?"

"I come with you."

"They told me to come alone. If they see you—"

"They won't," he snapped. "I'll stay out of sight on the floor in the back. Deal?"

I gave in, frantic to be going. "Okay—yes. Now *move—your—car.*"

He ran to pull the squad car far enough forward to clear my exit from the parking space, then clambered into the backseat through the passenger door of my rental as I slowed in swinging wide enough to avoid the police car that he'd left sitting behind two other vehicles.

"Get down," I told him. "They said not to bring police and may be watching."

His image vanished from the rearview mirror as he sank out of sight onto the floor. "What—?" he started to inquire, but again I interrupted.

"I'll explain it later," I told him, swinging around the plaza to an exit.

Two cars waiting for a break in traffic to make a left turn onto the street behind Charley's Corner had me honking my horn in aggravation before they finally moved and left the way clear for me to make a right. There was no parking along that street, so I pulled up with both left wheels on the sidewalk next to the Dumpster and hopped out, leaving Herrera in the back, forced to trust that he would do as promised and stay out of sight.

Looking carefully around, I saw no one who looked the least bit suspicious, so I cautiously approached the Dumpster, hoping to find Stretch inside. Once again pulling myself up to look inside, I was disappointed to see that it looked exactly as before, a small amount of trash cluttering its interior, but no rusty brown dachshund anywhere. Then, just as I was about to lower myself back to the ground, a black trash bag *moved*, rustling the plastic.

"*Stretch?*"

I was over the top and into the Dumpster in seconds, landing hard on another bag that had something in it that poked a hole and jabbed my leg. Ignoring it, I crawled across to the bag that had moved—and was moving again—and began to tear at it with both hands.

"Stretch, you darlin' dog. Are you in there?"

With a mighty yank, I tore the bag completely open down one side and, before I could retreat, a large rat came leaping free and scurried madly away to the far side of the Dumpster. I have no phobias concerning rats, but I do detest them for their stealth and filthy habits. Startled and repulsed, I watched it disappear into a pile of shredded paper. All disgust at the nasty creature was entirely forgotten, however, as I noticed that the package I had tossed in earlier still lay on top of that tangled pile.

So, for some reason, everything had not gone as planned. They had been late or had been prevented from retrieving the package.

Astonished, and before I could get up off my knees, I heard a vehicle coming fast and a squeal of tires as it stopped on the other side of the metal wall. I heard the vehicle door open, and someone stepped out and walked to the Dumpster. I looked up, expecting to see someone looking down, but no one appeared.

"Stay where you are and throw out the item, you stupid bitch," the telephone voice half whispered, in an attempt at disguise that wasn't so successful this time. It was definitely male.

Suddenly I'd had enough.

"Hand in my dog first."

"Come *on*," another male voice called from the vehicle. "Do the trade and let's get out of here."

"Not a chance," the one by the Dumpster told me. "Give it up or he's a done dog."

I heard Stretch yelp and whine as if he'd been hurt. It made me livid. Hurting innocent animals to make a point is never on my dance card and neither are people who do.

"Not until I have my dog back—alive and well—you sleazy bastard," I snapped, giving as good as I got verbally.

But it worked.

A pair of hands came into view above the top edge of the Dumpster and a growling Stretch was roughly hurled over. By throwing myself to one side in a major outfield play, I managed to catch him before he hit bottom. They had evidently not treated him well, for he snarled and snapped, not knowing who I was at first. Then he recognized me and whimpered, but stopped fighting and huddled as close as possible, glad to see me.

"Give it to me, or I'm coming in after it." The voice, louder and angrier now, was accompanied by the hands above the top again. This time one of them held a handgun. "You'll be sorry if I do."

"Here, then," I called, grabbed the package, and threw it beyond his reach, though I saw his hand lunge for it. With a thud, it hit what sounded like the hood of the vehicle. He swore and was gone after it.

In seconds the car door slammed shut and the engine roared as the vehicle raced away down the street.

Standing up carefully, hugging Stretch, I peered over the top of the Dumpster and caught a glimpse of a fast-moving black pickup disappearing around the corner.

When I turned back Herrera had climbed out of my car and was looking at me with an expression of rueful amazement.

"You are one gutsy woman who got extremely lucky, Ms. McNabb—very, very lucky. You both did."

In my euphoria at having my buddy back I guess I went a bit overboard, forgetting that Herrera had not been able to apprehend the kidnappers, as he clearly had intended to do.

He took Stretch as I climbed out of the Dumpster, ignoring the presence of the rat. I let him drive us back into the plaza to where his squad car was parked, while I held, examined, and comforted Stretch, noting that a bath for us both would take priority over anything else when we arrived home. Dumpster perfume might be appealing to a rat, but it would never be my choice of fragrance, and we both reeked of it.

# Twenty-three

Neither one of us got that clean immediately.

Herrera followed me home and I drove with Stretch in my lap, one hand on him almost the whole way as I told him what a brave dog he was and how glad I was to have him back.

He seemed to be uninjured but uncharacteristically nervous, and didn't want to ride by himself in the passenger seat. They had apparently not treated him as anything but an item for barter—maybe tied him up somewhere and mostly ignored him until he was useful. There were traces of adhesive on his muzzle and a whisker or two missing that led me to believe they had taped his mouth shut to keep him from making noise, as he would undoubtedly have told them loud and clear just what he thought of them with barks and growls. It made me angry, but also uneasy in wondering what their next move would be when they found they had been duped in their quest for whatever it was they had demanded.

Taking him inside the Winnebago, I gave him water and

food, which he attacked with a gusto that told me they hadn't bothered to feed him.

Herrera came in and sank into a seat at the dinette table as we both watched Stretch eat.

After a minute or two he straightened, pulled out his ever present notebook, and began his questions.

"So you found what they wanted. What was it you gave them?"

I turned from where I had knelt to watch Stretch practically inhale his food and gave Herrera a glance.

"I didn't find it. I gave them a book wrapped in newspaper and plastic. They couldn't see what it was until they opened it, so they didn't know it was fake."

He stared at me, scowling his disapproval. "Why, in the name of all that's holy, didn't you *call* me?"

"I didn't have time. They didn't call on my cell phone, as I expected. The call came in on the office phone and the manager came to get me."

"We knew that—it was the only other phone around, so we had it tapped—and yours was monitored as well. How did you think I knew where you were going?"

I had been so apprehensively focused on what I had been told to do and everything had happened so fast that I hadn't given his unexpected presence a second thought. Now I did, but it didn't make me feel better or more secure.

"What if they'd been watching the plaza and seen you?"

"I really didn't have much choice. Following you was all I could do quickly when I knew you were heading down there to do as they told you."

"What do you think they'll do when they find out I fooled them with the book? They're going to be angry," I said, looking down again at Stretch, who had finished every scrap of his food and come back to me. Picking him up, I rose and sat across from Herrera with an armful of smelly dog.

"I'm afraid they'll be more than just angry," he agreed. "So they'll be back, I think—probably in person this time. It's obviously something they want badly enough to risk a lot—must be either incriminating or pretty valuable."

"Why can't they just believe me when I tell them I haven't got—whatever *it* is?" I half wailed in aggravation. "Someone else must have it, or Shirley hid it somewhere safe that only she knew and nobody has it. I just want them to leave me alone."

"Listen," he said, leaning forward, elbows on table. "You're very vulnerable here in this RV. It's hard for us to guard without being detected if we want to catch them—and we do—and unsafe for you. If they could get inside *you* would make a much better and more serious hostage than your dog."

I thought about that and wasn't at all happy with the idea.

"You've got to remember that these people probably killed Shirley," he said abruptly. "Maybe the guy in the vat as well."

Remembering Shirley as we found her gave me the cold shivers. I stared at him without speaking, hugging Stretch until he began to squirm. Setting him on the floor, I watched him lie down, his nose on one of my feet, and look up at me with sleepy eyes. He was slow in getting his confidence back.

"If you're trying to scare me," I told Herrera finally, "it's working. I can't—no, I could, but I don't *want* to—stay here and be bait."

"No," he said. "You shouldn't, but we could move you to—"

"No," I interrupted, considering Stretch, as well as myself, and making a sudden decision for us both. "That won't be necessary. I'm going to leave—get both of us out of Taos. I can be ready to roll in an hour and I will be. It's time."

"You're going to run."

"Yes. I seldom run from anything, but I'm not dumb either, so I'm going to run now—a long ways. It's not worth staying."

Suddenly I felt that I had lost too many people that had been dear to me in my life—my parents, a brother and a sister, two husbands, and my best friend. I wasn't about to lose another, even if Stretch wasn't a human. And I for damn sure wasn't interested in being someone's hostage, or in getting myself hurt or killed.

I had become tangled in something that was really none of my business, that should not have concerned me, that I had been pulled into simply by being there, and that, aside from my own stubbornness, I could, and should, have left alone. It was time to get out of it.

"I understand," Herrera told me. "And you have every right to do just that, but here you at least have some protection. You have to understand that they might follow you, and if you're not in Taos you'll have none."

"They won't." Somehow I felt that gone was gone and I'd be okay once I was away from there. "But I'll wait and slip out in the dark, early tomorrow morning. I'm sorry I can't stay and help you catch these people. But I've told you everything I know and it's time to leave."

"Where will you go?"

"I haven't decided yet. North. Colorado probably."

"It would be wise to take the canyon road east. It's the closest way out of Taos from here and avoids the main street. Heading either north or south would mean a drive half the length of Paseo del Pueblo."

"I've driven the canyon road coming back on the Enchanted Circle. Beyond that it passes through Cimarron, then goes on to the border at Raton, where I can cross into Colorado."

He nodded soberly. "I can help a little, if you're really determined to go."

I assured him I was.

"I'll have someone here until you leave tonight. Then they can trail you into the canyon far enough to watch and make sure no one follows. If they see someone suspicious behind you, they'll stop them."

"I would appreciate that. And thank you for everything you've done for me."

There was little left to say. We looked at each other across the table.

"I wish I knew what they are so desperate to find," he said finally.

I nodded. So did I.

"What's your Yorkie's name again?" I asked.

"Puñado."

"What does it mean?"

" 'Handful'—which was all he was as a tiny puppy, and still is—especially in spirit. A real handful, in both senses of the word."

"Good name."

As soon as Herrera was gone I gave Stretch the scrubbing of his life, dried him off, then took a long, hot shower of my own, shampooing my hair and soaping up twice, till I was sure *eau de Dumpster* was a thing of the past. It felt marvelous and as if I had scrubbed off some of my apprehension along with the dirt.

True to his word, Herrera sent my guardian angel, Officer Jim Tolliver, back again to keep watch over me—outside the door this time. He knocked politely upon arriving to let me know he was on duty and I got out one of my folding lawn chairs from a compartment under the rig. There was no reason he shouldn't be comfortable at his job. I offered him lunch, but he showed me a cooler, which he said had food and sodas on ice, so I left him and went to take care of what needed to be done before I left Taos.

Checking to be sure I had enough gas to take me as far as Cimarron and would not need to fill up before leaving, I spent part of the afternoon getting the inside of the Winnebago prepared for travel. The outside water, electric, and sewer hookups I left to take care of quickly and after dark, just before I drove out.

When I'd done everything possible to get ready for the road, I called the office and told the manager I would be leaving and to put the bill on my credit card. Another call to the car rental company assured me they would pick up the car the next day and bill it similarly. Then I made a short trip to the grocery, where I stocked up for several days. Unwilling to let Stretch out of my sight, even for those few minutes, I took him along into the store, which earned me a frowning reprimand from a clerk at the checkout stand.

"We don't allow—" she began.

"Sorry," I told her. "Won't happen again."

I considered stopping in at Weaving Southwest to tell Pat I wouldn't be able to make it there for my lesson the next day, but something kept me from it—a feeling that I would be wise not to tell anyone else that I was leaving. Butch came to mind, but I decided I would call him later from somewhere down the road.

Stopping long enough at Bravo to pick up a sandwich, I went home and ate it for a late lunch, after which, having had little real sleep the night before and knowing I would be getting up very early to head for Cimarron, Stretch and I both took a two-hour nap.

As usual, I got out my maps and took a look at the route I planned to take the next day: to Cimarron, then north to Raton, and on into Colorado; I could make it to Colorado Springs in one day by driving late. But then my stubbornness kicked in again and I decided to spend the day in and around Cimarron and go on into Colorado on Tuesday. There was a lot of early western history in that area that interested me and I refused to miss it out of fear. Leaving was enough surrender to these jerks and con men. They could not have the rest of my life, which I intended to reclaim as soon as the lights of Taos had disappeared in my rearview mirror.

I have to admit that I felt a bit guilty about leaving, but I knew it was caused by stubborn ego and curiosity as much as anything. Herrera liked me, but it would probably be a relief to have me gone and not have to sidetrack one of his officers to stand senior citizen guard. Reminding myself that unreasonable obduracy can be a bad habit and that sometimes the better part of valor is to run like hell, I made myself stop thinking about it.

Going to bed early, I left a couple of lights on in the front part of the Winnebago and took Stretch with me into the bedroom. This time he went willingly to sleep in his basket by the bed and I was glad that he was feeling safe again. By ten o'clock we were both asleep and I didn't wake until the alarm I had set went off at half past three.

Knowing it would start to grow light about an hour later and the sun would rise around five o'clock, I dressed and went outside. Officer Tolliver helped me disconnect the hookups and stow the lines in their proper storage spaces under the Winnebago.

"I've called for the car so we can follow you into the canyon, Ms. McNabb," he told me. "It'll be here in a couple of minutes."

It was. I thanked him, got the motor running, and pulled out of the RV park, taking a right. Turning two more corners, I was on Pueblo del Canyon East, headed into Taos Canyon on my way to Cimarron, with a police escort close behind.

As the driver had explained, he and Tolliver would follow me for about ten miles, then pull over and watch to see that no one—especially a black pickup—was trailing along behind me. Beyond that we would continue on our own.

It worked exactly that way. He flashed his lights as they pulled onto a side road when we had gone almost ten miles, I tapped my brakes to let him know I had seen, and they disappeared behind me as I rounded a corner on the winding road. Though I often glanced at the rearview mirror for the next few miles, the road remained empty behind me. By the time I arrived in Cimarron the sun was up and I was feeling hopeful and quite confident that I had left the threats behind me.

But you just never know, do you?

# Twenty-four

Stretch and I had a pleasant, if watchful, day in and around Cimarron, which is a small, quietly historic town of around nine hundred souls in an area of about two square miles. The population, I learned, is almost 60 percent Hispanic, a significantly higher proportion than that of the rest of New Mexico. Looking out across the rolling hills that surround the town, I could imagine the prairie schooners of pioneer families and heavy freight wagons that came through in groups for protection from Indians during the great migration across the plains. So many passed along the Santa Fe Trail that their wagon tracks can still be seen.

I parked on the main street, which runs parallel to the highway, in front of a restaurant where I had breakfast, leaving Stretch in the motor home for the first time since I got him back. But always cautious, I took a seat at a table next to the window where I could keep a watchful eye on the Winnebago and the highway beyond it. It would be a while until I left behind the uneasiness that remained in my mind, though it seemed I had succeeded in leaving our threat behind in Taos.

When you consider, it is interesting how most of us spend our everyday lives without fear. There are hundreds of terrible things that could happen to us, or to those we care about, but we go along, innocently confident that everything will go well, or at least mostly according to plan, with the exception of minor irritating interruptions. But those are about all we are prepared for—not real disaster. So we are often ill-equipped to deal with it when it unexpectedly comes our way, as it had mine. And it takes a long time to resume the usual patterns of life without an apprehension lurking in the shadows of the mind that, in anticipation, keeps us alert to what might come, or come again.

Stretch and I were both feeling that sort of slowly fading low-grade anxiety. Still, though I remained vigilant—I am not thick enough to ignore it entirely—I was determined to enjoy Cimarron and whatever I found interesting without fleeing desperately north into Colorado.

After breakfast and visits to a couple of shops along the street, I took a side road south of town and drove till I found the St. James Hotel, with its haunted reputation. There I spent the night without a hint of spectral presence.

The next morning I had a leisurely breakfast and took us out of Cimarron, headed for the Colorado border. Not far across it, on what I thought was a whim, instead of going on to Colorado Springs, I turned left in Walsenburg and drove west, winding up at the Great Sand Dunes National Monument, a place I had longed to see. Entering the monument at close to noon, I parked the Winnebago at the visitor center, went in to get some information, and found Kris Illenberger, a friendly, helpful young man with a great smile, who directed me to several brochures, a video, and a book on the dunes, all of which I bought and took with me as I drove on to the campground that lay farther along the road.

As usual, before going out to sightsee, I took a look at the material I had gathered, so I would have some intelligent idea of what was around me on the walk I planned to take with Stretch. Remembering that I had picked up a book on Colorado at the Moby Dickens bookstore in Taos, I went to get it from the shelf where I keep my small collection of reading material, reminding myself that I had promised myself to send some of the books home to Alaska soon. As I carried it back to the dinette table, I remember half consciously thinking that the colorful dust jacket felt a little loose on the book, but I didn't examine it until I was sitting down again. Opening the cover, I was at first puzzled to find that the volume was not printed, but handwritten—not what I expected at all.

Closing the book and flipping the dust jacket off, I sat staring at the cover that was revealed. To my utter astonishment, there in front of me was the blue journal I had seen on Shirley's desk in the duplex—the one that I had virtuously resisted reading.

A book disguised as a book! She had used a classic means of hiding a thing in plain sight that had fooled me as well as those who had searched my motor home so thoroughly. No wonder they had been willing to accept the wrapped package I tossed at them from the Dumpster, for I had come closer than I knew in disguising one book for another. This journal was what they had really wanted, and there had to be a reason that they wanted it so badly. The only thing that made sense of their determination to recover it was that Shirley had written something incriminating in it—or at least they thought or were afraid she had.

This time I was not hesitant in reading her journal and there in the last few entries, along with her hurt and anger at Tony Cole's disappearance with the money she had loaned him, she poured out information, fears, suspicions, and names that shocked and startled me. Alan Medina's name was among them. One other was familiar and unexpected. They took me on a new and different track that I, and Herrera, had never considered.

My first impulse was to call him immediately, for he needed to know the things I had learned. Retrieving my cell phone, I tried. What stopped me was that from where I was located, in a valley between mountain ranges, I could not get a signal.

The eastern half of the United States is mostly covered in terms of cell phone service. Once you reach the mountains of the West, however, except for population centers and along main highways, service can be nonexistent, or spotty at best. In the hills that roll east of the Continental Divide, if you get a signal at all, the minute you go into a dip in the road the phone goes dead, and you are talking to the air.

I had no doubt now that I had escaped from the tangle of threats of Taos and I was comfortable where I was—feeling free once again. Does a bird let out of a cage regret abandoning its confinement enough to go back? Perhaps, depending on the circumstances, but I think not for long, and neither did I, having realized a total relief in being free. Guilt in staying where I was, or going even farther away, was setting in, however. And it seemed that the only way to get the information I had learned from Shirley's journal to Herrera quickly was to take it back where I had just come from.

I considered the possibility of driving to some location where I could get a signal for the cell phone, or finding a land line at the visitor center, but I knew that the journal itself, in her own handwriting, was a piece of evidence that not only proved Shirley had not killed herself but pointed fingers at those most likely responsible for her death, and possibly Anthony Cole's. Toss the thing in the mail? Possible. But by the time it reached Herrera the perpetrators could easily have scattered and left town. The more I considered the problem, the fewer options I knew I had.

Tangled up in all that, I knew it was not my style to cut and run from trouble, and I was feeling more than a bit foolish at compromising my principles. I knew what my Daniel would have cautioned: *Take care you don't let pride convince you that you're doing the right thing. Remember it goeth before a fall.*

*Right!*

I had left Stretch's leash on the opposite dinette seat and, as he sometimes does, he pulled it down and came with it in his mouth to stand and look up at me—a not so subtle reminder that I had promised him a walk and he needed one.

"Okay, lovie," I told him, getting up and reaching for the keys to the Winnebago. "We'll go walkabout. I can think about all this as we explore."

We walked a long way from the campground and were out among the dunes when the wind and rain drove us home later. I struggled with resistance to returning to Taos, knew I didn't want to continue to feel guilty, and finally made up my mind to do the right thing—with a few nudges in knowing what my Daniel would have thought and said about it.

At nine the next morning I put the motor home back on the road and drove south, crossed the border into New Mexico just above Costilla, and was soon back in the lovely Hondo Valley, passing through Questa once again, headed in the opposite direction this time.

With the discovery of the journal I was feeling more positive, though as we came closer to Taos a sense of possible danger rose in the back of my mind. We made Taos before noon, as planned, passing the Kachina Inn, where I remembered that I had intended to go to see the Indian dancing. Maybe this time I would.

As I came to Weaving Southwest I also remembered that I had not called Pat to cancel my class the day before. Wanting to call Herrera anyway, I decided that it would be as good a place to stop as any, for I could accomplish both things there.

One Winnebago motor home is pretty much like others, but mine has Alaska plates, which would be a dead giveaway to anyone looking. So rather than park out in front of the shop on Paseo del Pueblo Norte, I pulled into a lot at the end of the building, where the bright yellow rectangle would be less visible.

Before going in to see Pat I called Herrera, who was astonished that I was back, but when I told him that I had found what was lost he said he would be right over.

"You can tell me about it when I get there," he agreed.

Taking the journal with me in my bag and Stretch on his leash, I went around the corner from the parking lot and into Weaving Southwest, where I found Pat at her desk in the back. She was taking an order on the phone, so I used the time to admire the colorful shelves of yarn on the wall, then went to say hello to Mary Ann, who was unpacking a box of books onto a shelf toward the front of the shop.

"Hey," called Pat, coming to find me when she finished her phone call. "Missed you yesterday. Did I get the day wrong?"

I apologized and assured her she had not, but didn't go into detail about where I had been or why—simply said I had been unavoidably detained.

"Want to reschedule?" she asked.

"Let's wait till I know what would be a good time," I told her. "I'll call you."

"I drove by the RV park last night to invite you to dinner," she said, "but you weren't there and they said you had checked out. Did you move somewhere else?"

The question caught me off guard for a second or two.

"I spent some time in the Hondo Valley," I said finally— which was stretching the truth, as I was feeling a bit cornered. I hate prevarication, but sometimes it seems necessary and this was one of those times, though I wasn't quite sure why. Probably at that point I would have been cautious with anyone who asked questions about where I was going or had been.

She gave me a puzzled glance, clearly sensing my hesitation, then waved me to the rear where we could talk in private.

"What's going on?" she asked. "Does this have something to do with Shirley's death? I've been hearing rumors—thanks to Connie, of course—that the guy they found in Doris's dye vat was the one Shirley was seeing."

I should have remembered that this was a town, not a city, and that the rumor mill would grind fine and its chaff be widely and quickly spread on the wind of gossip.

Much of what had taken place in the last week seemed somehow to come back to connect with weaving one way or another—or at least with the people involved in weaving. I considered that for a minute. There was Weaving Southwest, where many weavers came and went; Connie, who seemed to consider it a perfect place to spread her rumors; a weaver's dye vat, where one body that was probably Anthony Cole had been found; Shirley, the other dead person, who was a weaver and had been involved with Cole; Alan Medina, who was not a weaver so far as I knew, but was connected to Shirley through that abstract in his gallery; and what else was there?

Glancing around the shop, where everything was connected to weaving, as I thought about the relationships between these things and people, my attention was caught by the rug Butch had selected at the opening of the show the Friday before. Suddenly I remembered the two woven pieces I had seen in the Medina Gallery that had reminded me of this one that had been woven by Ford Whitaker—another connection—not only because of his weaving but because he had admitted seeing Anthony Cole with Shirley, at the Taos Inn and elsewhere.

Ford Whitaker? Charmingly handsome, casually natural, seemingly trustworthy—Ford Whitaker? I caught my breath at the idea, remembering that when I was in the Dumpster a second man had called out from the pickup to the one who was holding Stretch: *"Come on. Do the trade and let's get out of here."* Could it possibly have been . . .

"What is it?" Pat asked. "You don't look so good."

Before I could answer, or decide if I wanted to, the door opened and Herrera came hurrying in.

Seeing me with Pat at the back of the shop, he came to us in long strides.

"Ms. McNabb," he said.

"Maxie," I reminded him. "Just Maxie, please."

He grinned. "Okay—*Maxie*. Hi there, Stretch."

The dog trotted to the end of the leash I was holding and looked up expectantly, wagging his tail with pleasure at reuniting with what he knew was a friend.

Herrera knelt to give him a quick bit of hands-on affection.

I was breathing again, having decided that, considering the connections with weaving, it would be good to have Pat on our side. She was familiar with all the local weavers personally and could be a good source of information that neither Herrera nor I could know or find out.

It was a decision neither of us would regret.

# Twenty-five

Rather than talk in Pat's office where we would be interrupted, the three of us went to the Winnebago in the parking lot next door. There I gave Herrera Shirley's journal and while he read through the significant parts of it I began to tell Pat what had been going on in the last few days.

"Well," she said, when I had sketched out the major happenings along with some of our assumptions and suspicions. "I can help get answers to some of the things you want to know. Let me think about all this. But you've got another problem to solve first. It's pretty obvious you shouldn't go back to that RV park. It would be like hanging out a sign that you're back in Taos. You might as well let these people continue to think you're not here, so for the time being why don't you come and park next to my place? We can rig an electric line and there's outside water to hook up to already."

"That's a very good idea," Herrera, who had finished examining most of the journal, agreed. "I was just considering how to make you invisible—not easy with a motor home this big."

"It's only thirty feet long," I told him. "There are lots that are much bigger."

"Then I'm glad you aren't driving one of those." He smiled, then turned serious. "This journal of Shirley's has got to be what Medina and his cohorts were looking for. It identifies him and Cole, of course, and mentions two more in passing who might be connected."

"Who?" asked Pat. "It's a small town, so it could be someone I know."

"I think I'd better check one of them out before we take it any further," he said, giving me a look that meant I should keep the name to myself as well. What you *can* do is tell me what you know of Ford Whitaker."

*"Ford?"* Pat's eyes widened. "Surely you can't think that Ford has anything to do with any of this? I don't know anything that would help you one way or another, but everybody likes him. He's a great person and a fine weaver."

"Fine weaver or not, his name appears in this journal as somebody Shirley had questions about. Evidently he wasn't too happy when she took up with Cole."

Letting it go for the time being, though I knew he had no intention of ignoring it, he paused and turned to me.

"By the way, we are sure now that the body found in the vat was Cole's—or, as I told you the other day, Earl Jones, who was using "Anthony Cole" as an alias, among others. And I still have that hundred-thousand-dollar motive in mind. But it's also possible that someone else killed them both, wanting it to look like Shirley killed him, then took her own life."

"So Shirley really didn't kill herself?" Pat asked.

"No," Herrera told her. "But I thought she might have killed Jones—or Cole, as you knew him."

"Why?"

It was something I hadn't explained, so we told her about the stolen money and how upset Shirley had been about it.

"What happened to the money?" I asked.

Herrera shook his head. "I don't have an answer to that yet. The check she gave him was cashed, but what he did with the money we have no way of knowing. It's always possible that he was killed for it, so I'm keeping that in mind. A hundred thousand dollars goes a long way as motivation for murder."

He was right, of course. Still, I couldn't help thinking that there were easier and more permanent ways to dispose of a body than dumping it into a vat full of water. That it was sure to be found made you think the killer had meant to make a point of some kind by putting it there.

"Was he dead when he was put into the vat?" I asked. "Or did he drown?"

Pat gave me a glance that told me she thought the question ghoulish but interesting.

"Not much gets past you, does it, Ms. M?" Herrera said, a slight smile lifting the corners of his mouth.

"We are sure that Doris Matthews, the woman who owned the vat, had nothing to do with it. Whoever did it not only wanted him to be found but wanted him to know he was going to die. His hands and feet were tied together behind his back, so he couldn't get leverage to stand, and his mouth was taped shut, so he couldn't make a lot of noise. Then he was methodically held under water over and over again until he finally couldn't hold his breath any longer and drowned—which may have been an attempt to make him tell where the money was. We think it happened that way because of the number of bruises on his head and shoulders and the force with which they were made in holding him down.

"He struggled as much as he could, for as long as he could. It wasn't a quick or merciful way to die. I'm inclined to believe that whoever wanted him dead also had vengeance as a motive, which is why the stolen money made me look at Shirley for it."

"Wait a minute," Pat said, suddenly sitting up straight and turning to Herrera. "That's the second time you've said you 'looked at Shirley'—as in the past tense: you said you 'thought she might have' killed him and that 'the money made' you 'look at' her." Does that mean you don't think she killed him anymore?"

"Very perceptive," he answered, nodding. "Maxie, do you remember my telling you what we learned about the finger-prints we found after your break-in?"

"Sure."

"Well, the same prints were found again—on and around the vat where the guy was drowned. Now that we have Shirley's body to compare them to we know that they're not hers."

"Whose are they?" Pat asked.

"They belong to another woman—a Sharon Beil. Ever hear of her?"

"No. Who is she?"

"A woman with a record in California."

"Shirley said she was from California. Did this Beil woman kill Shirley too?"

"Good question," Herrera told her, reaching to pat Stretch, who had curled up next to him on the dinette bench.

He soon went off with the journal to do some further sleuthing both in and out of its pages.

———

Pat left Mary Ann in charge of Weaving Southwest and drove ahead of me to her place by a back road rather than through downtown Taos. As she had said, it was a much better place to park the Winnebago, pretty much off the beaten track and out of sight, where few people would ever think to look for a motor home. I was soon hooked up to water and electricity and had been offered the use of her kitchen and bathroom.

I called the car rental agency and had them bring me another compact car, so I had wheels, just in case I needed them. Having an anonymous mode of transportation wasn't a bad idea, considering that the Winnebago was large and obvious with its Alaska plates.

We sat down with a cup of tea and I had just started to fill Pat in on a few more details of Shirley's death when the cell phone in my bag rang. Still a little nervous from waiting for the kidnappers to call, I was startled.

Hesitantly, I answered it, thinking it might be Herrera. "Yes?"

"Hey! There you are—finally. Where've you been? I've been trying to reach you since sometime yesterday," Butch Stringer's voice said in my ear.

My breathing slowed and my blood pressure dropped back to its normal level.

"Would you believe I've been to Cimarron and the Great Sand Dunes in Colorado?" I asked. "It's been an interesting couple of days."

"Side trips, huh? Did you see the Tooth of Time in Cimarron—well, just outside of Cimarron? It's up behind the Philmont Scout Ranch on part of their land south of town."

"What the heck is the Tooth of Time?"

"An awesome formation on a ridge of the Sangre de Cristos that looks like a tooth. It was a landmark for the early pioneers. You really should take the time to see it if you go through there again."

"I'll remember that. Where are you?"

"Still in Santa Fe. The run I was supposed to make to Phoenix got canceled because the customer added something to the load and it isn't going to be ready till early next week. Thought if you were going to be around and wouldn't mind company I'd take a couple of days off, come back up Thursday and stay till Sunday."

I assured him I'd enjoy his company and feel much safer with Butch than on my own.

"Any news on your break-in? You haven't had any more, have you?"

"Well, now that you mention it, there was something else that happened, but it's okay now."

"What happened?"

"I'll tell you about it when you come up."

"Are you all right?"

"Yes, I'm fine, but I'm not at the RV park. I'm parked outside Pat Dozier's house. You remember her from Weaving Southwest?"

"Sure. Listen—have they caught whoever did it? No? Okay, that's it. You can expect me before noon tomorrow. I'm not waiting till Thursday. How can I find you?"

I handed the phone to Pat and she gave him directions.

"What a nice man," she said, when she had broken the connection.

I agreed, feeling a huge relief at knowing I would soon have Butch as backup again.

It is truly amazing how much stress you can feel and not realize it until it begins to go away. I had felt very stressed when I left Taos, but as I went farther west it had lessened and was almost gone by the time I arrived in Colorado. I had picked a lot of it up again in coming back, but once again I refused to surrender to it.

"What do you know about a landmark called the Tooth of Time?" I asked Pat. "Butch says I should go and see it when I go through Cimarron again."

"Oh, you should. It's a pretty impressive hunk of rock that crowns the ridge behind the Philmont Scout Ranch and is sort of a symbol for them. They use it on pins and badges, and take Scouts on hikes up to it. Someone told me once that they tell the boys that if they look over their shoulder at it before leaving they're sure to come back sometime."

"Who named it?"

"I have no idea, but it's a good one."

It was—and, probably because we had been talking about Shirley, it reminded me of how determined she had seemed to appear younger than she actually was—avoiding the bite that time and getting older have for most of us seniors in one way or another. Filing away a mental reminder to search out that rock sometime in the near future, I let it go for the moment and asked Pat about the big loom and shelves of yarn and other weaving supplies that took up a significant portion of her two-story residence, which was not large, but suited her well.

She showed me around, including her small backyard surrounded by another coyote fence, where she had a large kettle that sat on a rack over a propane burner to heat water for dyeing her own yarn. It was much smaller than Bettye Sullivan's, but large enough to hold water and yarn for the purposes of a single weaver.

"I think," I told her, "that I'll be glad to leave the dyeing to you and buy my yarn from a great shop I have discovered in Taos."

She laughed and said they would be happy to fill any orders I might have.

"Why don't you get your loom and I'll get you started on what we were going to do yesterday," she suggested.

So I retrieved it from the Winnebago and, after showing me what to do, she went to her own loom and we spent the afternoon happily weaving, while Stretch explored or took naps, ignoring and ignored by Pat's fluffy cat.

# Twenty-six

It is amazing how complacent you can get when you feel secure.

Pat and I had gone to bed quite early, having heard no more from Herrera. It was comforting to have my own living space parked in a place I felt was out of harm's way, and I appreciated it. Stretch and I had climbed into the Winnebago, I locked up, closed all the curtains and blinds, and we readied ourselves for the night. I turned out the lights and everything was quiet as I drifted off to sleep feeling fairly confident.

But just when you think you're safe . . .

It was dark. Except for one thin finger of dim light that slipped in from a distant streetlamp through the narrow edge of a window blind, the bedroom space was inky blackness.

I woke abruptly, already sitting up in bed, my heart pounding as I listened intently, alert for a repetition of the small, surreptitious sound I had heard, almost felt, in my sleep. A dream? Possibly, but I thought not, for it seemed to have none of the hallmarks of a dream and all of those of reality.

Stretch whined softly from his basket, but did not bark or go running forward, as he would normally have done to confront any intruder prowling outside. That small sound from him seemed odd, but not unreasonable, I thought, given that he would probably be shy for a while after his ill treatment at the hands of strangers.

I sat perfectly still, listening for another sound and waiting to feel any motion at all in the motor home. But I knew that I had stabilized it when I parked next to Pat's and there would be little or no motion if someone were cautious enough to step inside slowly and carefully.

Nothing.

Then, almost in the air against my skin, there was a hint of movement without a sound of any kind and I was instantly aware that someone besides Stretch and myself was a part of the extreme darkness. That slim finger of light was broken as someone passed in front of it, then it returned whole, and I was able to just make out a vague silhouette of someone standing at the foot of my bed.

I froze, my breath caught in my throat.

How had this person, whoever it was, gotten in?

Before going to Cimarron I had returned the shotgun to its normal traveling location in my secret hiding space and had not taken it out again, feeling more secure parked outside Pat's place. Now I fervently wished that it were within reach. A frightened senior woman holding a shotgun pointed at me with trembling hands is nothing in front of which I'd want to stand. But I had nothing but a pillow to throw at whoever it was that was standing there so close.

Stretch whimpered and moved, but did not leave his basket.

I wished he had been sleeping on my bed, where I could

have reached a hand to reassure him. Instead I forced myself to take a deep breath.

"Who's there?" I asked in a voice that, to my relief, came out sounding more confident than I was feeling, so, with a bit of bravado, I added, "And what the hell do you want?"

There was a long moment of silence, then a soft voice instructed, "Turn on a light."

I fumbled to locate the switch for the overhead reading light and turned it on.

*Shirley Morgan*—the woman I knew was dead because I had found her body in a bathtub full of bloody water—*was standing at the foot of my bed.*

I was so shocked I could do nothing but stare at her, blinking like an owl, my mouth open even wider than my eyes, as my brain stripped gears in an attempt to rationalize her reality.

"What have you done with my sister's diary?" she asked.

"Diary?" I managed to croak out, trying to see if this specter had a weapon. Her hands were empty.

It was beginning to dawn on me that this was not Shirley, though seen in half-light it looked so much like her it was terrifying. This had to be the older woman whose picture Herrera had showed me several days before, who I had thought might have been Shirley before a face-lift. *Sharon,* I remembered— *Sharon Beil.*

She was fairly tall, a strong-looking woman in her late fifties or early sixties with large, square hands. Her hair was brown, not bleached as Shirley's had been. Her face was attractive, slightly different from Shirley's in shape but otherwise similar, especially the eyes. Though she couldn't look so much like Shirley and not be her sister, no face-lift had made her look younger than her actual age, but she was clearly the older of the two.

She looked tired and unhappy, but there was a hint of inflexible determination and resolve in the way she held herself and looked steadily at me.

How she had found me, I had no idea.

"Her diary—her blue journal. Where is it?" she demanded.

Now that it was no longer in my possession there was no reason not to tell her, was there?

"The police inspector has it. Shirley hid it here, but I found it and gave it to him yesterday."

"You're sure?"

"Of course I'm sure."

She sighed as if relieved and sat down suddenly on the foot of the bed.

"Good. Then he'll know who to look for."

"Who?" I asked.

She simply shook her head. "He'll know. And he'll find them."

"He's already looking."

"You know who I am?" she asked.

"I think I do. You're Shirley's sister, Sharon."

"Yes, I am. And thank you," she said, unexpectedly.

"For what?"

"For giving the diary to him and for taking care of my little sister when I couldn't."

"All I did was take her home from the hospital that day. She only stayed with me one night before she disappeared. I still don't understand why."

"I know, but it kept her alive long enough to hide the journal here, where she hoped no one would think to look. They did, but she must have done a good job, because they didn't find it, did they? And I couldn't find it either. Where did she hide it, by the way?"

I told her about finding it disguised in the wrong book cover.

"It was clever enough to fool whoever tore this place apart looking for it."

Sharon nodded sadly. "She always was the clever one, my baby sister—except about men. She was never clever about men—always too trusting and gullible."

I thought about the ways I knew that was true.

Stretch, following my lead, had accepted her presence and gone back to sleep.

As she stood up again, he woke, wagged his tail, and looked up at her.

"Hello there," she said to him. Then to me, "I have to go. You can tell your policeman that I was here if you like. I won't be staying in Taos more than a few hours. Except for one thing, I've done what I came here for."

"What is that?"

I couldn't resist asking, but she gave me an odd sort of smile and turned to leave.

"Wait," I said. "Does anyone else know where I am? How did you find me?"

"I don't know if they do, but it wasn't that hard," she said, gave me a quick nod, and left the bedroom without another word.

I heard the coach door close a moment or two later.

When I went to lock it and looked outside, she was nowhere to be seen, but the key I had found missing after the break-in had been carefully laid on the countertop in the galley. Had she, then, been the person who tore apart my living space? If so, who had been with her and why had they worn gloves when she hadn't?

I put the key on the hook where it belonged and went back to bed, where I lay awake for some time, thinking—wishing for answers I still didn't have.

The next morning Pat came to give me a key to her house and stayed for a quick cup of coffee before going to work at Weaving Southwest. I didn't tell her about my middle-of-the-night visitor, preferring to keep it to myself for the time being.

"I'll be back about four," she said as she left. "Call me if you need—well, help, or anything."

I promised I would and waved her off from the door of the Winnebago.

It was a sunny morning, but one by one dark clouds that looked as if they might hold rain were creeping in over the mountains. Far out over the mesa west of town I could see several that were already releasing the water they carried as they moved slowly along, but much of it seemed to be evaporating before it ever reached the ground. *Walking rain,* I thought, remembering that I had wondered at the term, but now it made perfect sense.

There were no trees near Pat's house and, therefore, no birds hanging out in them like the ones in the RV park that had warbled cheerfully overhead in the mornings. I missed them, but felt it was worth their absence in trade for the security of my current location.

Turning on the radio, I found a station that was playing Western music, retrieved my weaving from inside Pat's house, and sat down to see what I could do without a handy coach, while I waited for Butch Stringer to arrive. It was pleasant work, especially with those wonderful yarns, easy on the hands and mind, slightly hypnotic, but not as much so as the rhythmic sounds of the pedal loom we had watched Kelly use at the shop. Still, I found a rhythm of my own that went along nicely to Luckenbach, Texas, with Waylon and Willie and the boys.

I had thought of calling Herrera to tell him about my midnight visit from Sharon Beil, but something kept me from it. Now that she was gone—and evidently intended to go much farther away—I found myself thinking about her and considering what he had said about her fingerprints on and around the vat where Tony Cole—in another of those senior moments I couldn't remember his real name—had been killed. Had I made a mistake? She had said I could tell him or not, intimating that it didn't—or soon wouldn't—matter to her. Did she already have a plan in place that would allow her to disappear? It seemed so, for from the little I now knew, she didn't seem the sort to give up easily.

There had evidently been a bond between the two sisters, though they seemed unlike in several significant ways. Still, a sister is a sister; such a bond can be very strong, even if they don't agree on just how to spend their lives. I had a feeling I'd have liked to know Sharon better.

I took Stretch for a morning walk on a road toward the mountains, but we had to hurry home under a sudden shower that, almost impishly, decided to walk with and on us, reaching the ground, but lightly.

Stretch barked at the postman who showed up at ten o'clock and dropped a couple of letters in Pat's mailbox, so I knew he was almost back to normal and ready again to challenge the world if appropriate. He too is a survivor and, in dog years, as much a senior citizen as I am.

All in all, it was probably the quietest morning I'd spent since arriving in Taos and I appreciated it as a time to breathe between storms of one kind or another, though I hoped Herrera's work would be successful and there wouldn't be another on the way.

I heard Butch arrive in his pickup shortly before noon and stepped out to welcome him back to Taos, very glad to see him again.

Over lunch I told him everything I could think of that had happened since he'd left to go back to Santa Fe—could it possibly have been only four days since we had gone to Bettye's on the mesa to see how she dyed yarn?

There was no way of knowing that the next couple of days would make me glad of that morning's quiet as storm clouds of quite another and more threatening kind would gather ominously and be upon us very soon.

# TWENTY-SEVEN

THERE WERE SO MANY PIECES TO THE PUZZLE THAT NOW, as I look back on it, I wonder at how we managed to fit many of them together at all.

Butch and I were sitting at the dinette table with the remains of lunch when Herrera drove up outside in a squad car and came in with a surprise riding on his arm.

When Stretch trotted quickly across to greet him, Herrera cautiously, making sure they wouldn't quarrel, set his tiny Yorkshire terrier down on the floor and we watched in amusement as the two little dogs circled and sniffed, getting acquainted.

"Puñado, this is Stretch," Herrera said, hunkering down to give each of them a pat, which they ignored in preference to their interest in each other.

"That's a pretty fierce police dog," Butch commented with a grin as he stood up to shake hands with Herrera.

"Well, he thinks he is anyway. Don't disabuse him of the idea. I wouldn't want to turn him into a wimp. You should see him cow Officer Tolliver's German shepherd, who can't figure out what to do about anything this small."

Once at ease with a new friend, Puñado scampered off, his tiny legs a blur of motion, to explore the Winnebago from stem to stern, Stretch padding proprietarily along behind.

When the three of us were settled with fresh coffee, I told Herrera about my visitor in the dark of the night. He listened carefully, frowning.

"I've been close to catching up to her a couple of times," he said thoughtfully. "You say she didn't threaten you in any way?"

"No. She only wanted to know about the journal, and she was relieved to know that I had given it to you."

"That makes some sense, for because of it I now have Alan Medina in temporary custody, though he's not talking, except to swear that he had nothing to do with the killing of either Shirley Morgan or Earl Jones, aka Anthony Cole. The painting you saw in Shirley's apartment and then again in the gallery? He says he let Cole take it for a few days on speculation, but that Cole decided not to buy it and brought it back sometime before the end of last week. But in the journal Shirley says it was a gift to her from Cole."

"She told me it was a gift, but she didn't mention *him*."

"Medina also says he doesn't know Ford Whitaker and had nothing to do with the two of Whitaker's woven pieces you saw in the gallery. He says that his mother made all the arrangements for them. I have trouble with that because this is a small, tight community with lots of artists and most of them know each other, or at least know *of* each other. How can you show an artist in your gallery and not know something?"

"Did you ask Ford?"

"He's evidently gone to take some of his work to Santa Fe. Won't be back till tomorrow or Friday."

"He called me this morning and said he'd be back tomorrow," an unexpected voice informed us as the screen door opened and Pat climbed in. "He took two tapestries along with him to deliver for me—one of mine and one of Bettye Sullivan's. Hey, Butch. Good to see you. And, speaking of Ford, I just rolled the rug you bought at the show and wrapped it for transport. You can pick it up anytime you like, since you're here . . ."

That pretty much broke up the discussion.

Herrera took Puñado to ride in the squad car, leaving Stretch with his nose against the screen door, looking after them as if he'd been abandoned. In a world of motor-home-traveling Labradors and shepherds, there aren't many dogs around even close to his size, and he refuses to play with the likes of toy poodles or any breed that resembles a yapping, walking dust mop, which he views as an infringement upon his dignity.

Pat took a look at the weaving I had done and pronounced it acceptable, then showed me a trick or two about how to change colors or kinds of yarn. "You could be really good at this with a little practice," she told me.

Still tired from the interruption of my sleep the night before, I decided to take a nap. So I apologized to Butch, and he followed Pat off to the shop to claim his rug.

"No problem," he told me. "Call me when you wake up and I'll come back and we can decide what to do about dinner."

I was snoozing peacefully when the thunderstorm rolled in and began to pour rain on the roof of the Winnebago with a roar that woke me and sent me hurrying to close the overhead vents and a window I had left open. The sunshine had disappeared and overhead were none of the small, rather puffy, singular clouds that I had watched earlier as they walked thin rain across the distant mesa. Instead, the sky had grown a much darker charcoal gray in the form of a solid bank of heavy clouds that were now dumping water on Taos with a vengeance. It probably wouldn't last long, but it had pulled out all the timpani and cymbals and the rest of the percussion. Thunder rolled, lightning flashed, and Stretch, unused to such a cacophony, came to curl up next to my feet under the table as I sat watching the torrent out the window. A sudden wind buffeted the motor home so that I could feel each gust, even though the stabilizers were in place.

As it began to quiet down to a more gentle rain, I went back and lay down on my bed, taking Stretch with me. He settled at my feet and was soon wheezing, as he sometimes does, but I couldn't get back to sleep for thinking things over again.

So Herrera had caught up with Alan Medina, but was getting nothing but denials out of him. I remembered how fast he had exited the gallery once he knew I was there. Why would he have all but fled from me if he weren't involved somehow—as he claimed he wasn't? I had never heard him speak, but Herrera thought it was Medina's voice that I had heard calling from the black pickup to the man who had tossed Stretch into the Dumpster behind Charley's Corner. Who was that man? Had the two of them killed Shirley? If so, why?

There were so many unanswered questions. I found I was still feeling glad to have met Shirley's sister, Sharon. If her fingerprints on Doris Matthews's dye vat were an indication that she had drowned Tony Cole—and I had to admit that I could think of no other reason they would have been found there—then a part of me hoped she would, as she had said, leave Taos and disappear. Maybe he didn't deserve to die for his con games, but he had certainly asked for it, especially from an unforgiving sister. Had he killed Shirley? No, I reminded myself, he had died first. Then who had killed her—and tried to make it look like a second and finally successful attempt at suicide?

I thought back to that bloody bathroom scene. Had there been anything at all to give us a clue? Closing my eyes, I tried to visualize it as I had found it, beginning with opening the door. There had been a towel on the toilet seat near the tub in which she died. What else? I remembered that Ann Barnes's threatening to be sick had interrupted my examination of the room. This long afterward, it was difficult to recall anything that I had overlooked at the time. Parts of the room remained a blank. Had there been soap in the tray by the tub? Had the medicine chest door been open, even a little? I had no idea.

My focus had been primarily on the body in the water, for obvious reasons. I could envision that with no trouble and wished I could not, for it was an ugly scene. It swam clearly into memory, the face with eyes staring upward, arms extended along her sides, hands palm up, and the horrible cuts that started at the wrist and continued vertically up her arms almost to the elbows. Why had her killer found it necessary to make such long, deep cuts? It must have been extremely painful, but there had been no indication that she had been restrained, or that she had struggled with her attacker. Except for the bruises on her ankles, there had been no sign that she had been held down by force. Could she have been drugged?

Shirley's murder had not been the result of a sudden impulse by her killer. Her supposed second and successful attempt

at suicide had been very well planned and executed—perhaps
too well.

Without consciously registering it at the time, I suddenly remembered that I had seen and recorded a thing that her killer
had overlooked. To make it seem that Shirley had butchered her
own arms, allowing herself to bleed to death, there should have
been something left near at hand that she would have used to
make the cuts. There had been nothing sharp within reach of
that tub—no knife, no razor blade, nothing at all that I could
remember. The police had found nothing in the tub with her
body. So she could not have cut her own arms and there was no
blood anywhere but in the tub. It must have been done there.

Herrera had said that they would have the results of the
postmortem in about a week. Shirley had died on a Friday.
Could it possibly have been only five days ago? Would he know
yet if she had been drugged? If so, he hadn't mentioned it.

I sat up, wondering about Ann Barnes, and realized that I
had not given her a thought since we found Shirley dead. She
had been upset enough to be sick, but how had she been taking
it all since then? *Poor lonely soul,* I thought. She might not be
terribly likeable, but living alone couldn't be easy for her, without a family. No wonder she kept such close watch on whoever
rented the place next door.

Guiltily, I knew I could, and should, have checked in on
her. It wouldn't hurt to do so now, and with the rental car I
had the means to do it. Herrera had Alan Medina supposedly
walking a narrow line in answering his questions and would, I
imagined, probably soon have the name of his confederate in
the kidnapping of Stretch, so I would most likely be safe if I
used the back roads to reach the duplex.

It had been almost two hours since Butch left with Pat. I thought about calling him, but decided that I wouldn't be gone long and would make the call when I came back.

Instead I wrote him a quick note, just in case he returned before I did. Then I took Stretch in the rental car and the long way around to Ann Barnes's, where I left him in the car and went up the walk, expecting to spend only a few minutes.

Once again the curtain twitched after I knocked on the door, but she opened it almost immediately.

"Oh, Mrs. McNabb!" she said with a surprised and pleased expression. "I was just wondering about you. Come in. Come right in."

"I can't stay," I told her, stepping in far enough to allow her to close the door behind me. "I just thought I'd be sure you were all right after—ah—the other day."

"Oh yes, I'm fine." She led the way across to her table next to the kitchen. "I'm just having a glass of iced tea. Please have one with me, will you?"

I really didn't want the tea, but she was patently anxious for company, so I agreed and took the chair she had pulled out and was waving me into. "Shirley told me you make fruit-flavored tea that is very good."

"Oh, I think I do, but the proof is in the tasting," she said from the kitchen, from which I heard the clink of ice and the pouring of liquid. Setting a tall, frosty glass of pinkish-brown tea and several ice cubes down in front of me, she smiled. "This is raspberry. Try it."

I did and found that Shirley had been half right. It was good, but a little too sweet, as many people seem to prefer their flavored teas, and had a faint bitter aftertaste, as if she had steeped it too long. "It's lovely, thank you."

"How nice of you to stop to see me," Ann smiled, sitting down across from me at the table. "And how are you and your little dog doing? It was such a horrid experience—finding her that way—wasn't it? The poor dear girl. And she was such a good tenant, too."

"Will you rent the place next door again soon?"

"Oh, I shall have to," she said, frowning slightly. "I depend on it so. Along with my Social Security, that income is all I have to keep me going. I must get someone to come in and clean the bathroom, though. I would be sick again if I tried to do it myself."

"No help from family?" I asked, curious, and took a long swallow of my tea, hoping to finish it quickly and be on my way before she could refill the glass.

"Oh, no. All my family is dead—now," she said softly, with an odd hesitation and a glance across the room. "I'm all by myself. But that's all right—I get by one way or another."

Interesting, I thought, how at a certain age some women simply retreat into a comfortable cave of their own making and avoid the world and other people. How old was she, anyway?

I had something in my eye, and rubbed at it with the back of one hand.

My glass of tea was almost empty, so I reached to finish it and was startled when my fingers hit it and knocked it over. The remaining liquid, along with the ice, spilled out across the table, leaving a brownish-pink stain on the embroidered cloth. I stared at it, wondering why I was suddenly so clumsy.

"Oh," I said. "I'm sho shorry. How mumsy of me."

Blinking in an attempt to clear away the haze that had somehow settled in between us, I watched the pattern of the tablecloth writhe and blur. What the hell was going on?

The sound as the glass rolled off the table and shattered on the floor startled me enough for a realization.

How could I have been so stupid?

*The woman has poisoned me!*

I peered across at her, everything faded, and I felt myself falling out of the chair. Elsewhere in the room there was some kind of crash as blackness settled in, but the last thing I remember was her wide grin—and the straight razor in her hand.

# Twenty-eight

AFTER A GOOD DINNER, PAT, FORD, HERRERA, BUTCH, and I sat together around a table on the outside patio at the Taos Inn, drinking margaritas and watching the younger crowd cruise by on Paseo del Pueblo Norte, like kids anywhere on Friday night. Between their calls to each other, and to others who sat at tables around us on the patio, I could hear some fine flamenco music that was being played by a seriously talented guitarist in the Adobe Bar behind us.

We were a cheerful and compatible group. I was feeling much relieved at knowing that everyone—including me—was safe and that our questions had been, or were being, answered. How different from Ann Barnes, a woman alone in a world she held at arm's length and couldn't help seeing as hostile, for to her way of thinking, piece by piece it had taken everything from her that she cherished. I thought back to my visit with her, looked around the table, and knew how lucky I was to be sitting there at all, alive and well, with people who cared for me and for whom I cared.

———

I had come slowly awake in a hospital hours after I fell from the chair at Ann's table and opened my eyes to find Butch Stringer asleep in a chair next to my bed. As I moved he woke, sat up, and leaned toward me with a huge smile.

"There you are finally," he said. "How do you feel?"

I thought about it, then tried to answer, but my throat hurt, so I nodded and croaked out, "Why is my throat so sore?"

"They pumped your stomach," he told me, reaching for a glass on the table by my bed. "Here. Have a drink of water."

He held it while I took a sip through a straw that had an accordion bend in it. That helped.

"What happened?"

"Do you remember being at the Barnes woman's house?" he asked.

Some confused pictures crowded into my mind of someone yelling, a brown stain spreading across the top of a table, and the crash of glass breaking.

"I went to see if she was okay," I said, remembering as I tried to sit up and noticed for the first time that I had an IV in my left arm.

Butch helped, tucking a second pillow behind me, and then sat back down.

"She put something in the tea she gave me," I recalled suddenly.

"She certainly did. The same stuff she gave Shirley Morgan to knock her out before she killed her."

"Oh dear. Why?"

"Why you? She thought you knew about Shirley."

"No. I mean why Shirley?"

A nurse opened the door and came in before he could answer.

While we watched, she checked my pulse and did the things you would expect with a thermometer and a blood pressure cuff, saying the sort of things you can imagine while she did them.

When she finished, she smiled and removed the IV.

"You're fine now, Mrs. McNabb," she assured me. "You can go home as soon as the doctor has a look. He'll be here in just a few minutes."

He was, and declared me fit to travel.

And right behind him came Herrera.

"So," he said. "I should have known you wouldn't leave the investigating to me. We were very lucky you left a note telling Butch where you were going. What were you *thinking* to go there alone?"

So that was how they had found and saved me.

"I went to see if she was all right," I told him. "It never crossed my mind that she had—that she really would . . ."

I let it go unfinished, as I recalled that my thoughts had been all around the truth before I left the Winnebago, following my own guilty impulse. I should have considered it a bit longer, shouldn't I?

It had been right there in front of us. So how had we missed it so completely?

Somehow I think most people may assume that senior citizens are less inclined to revenge, leaving murder to younger people with more physical ability, who have yet to establish complete control over their impulses and the possible consequences. We forget that older people have had longer to generate and adhere to our resentments and hatreds, and some may have learned subtle and effective, if not lethal, methods of expressing them. Practice makes perfect? Time may have teeth for oldies, but they can have teeth of their own. Ann certainly did.

"Why did she kill Shirley?" I asked Herrera.

"She thought Shirley had killed her son. Anthony Cole—Earle Jones—was a child she bore out of wedlock, before she married an Edward Barnes, now deceased. She and her son were in it together, you see. Part of the profits he conned out of rich widows and divorcées went to his mother. The arrangement with the door between the two units of the duplex simply made it easier for her to keep an eye on the women he encouraged to move into the place. Ann could go in and search their things for helpful information. It also made it easier for her to drag Shirley through and murder her in her own bathroom. Who would suspect an old lady, after all?"

I thought about that for a long minute and decided not to explain my ideas on the reality of senior citizenship to him or to take that remark personally. He would learn all that in time, as he met its teeth for himself.

"So you knew about it before today?" I asked.

"I suspected."

"Should have known you weren't telling me everything."

"Well, Ms. McNabb, I *am* a police officer, after all."

"Maxie, please," I reminded him.

Butch chuckled from his place in the chair.

"Time to take you home, I think," he said with a grin as he stood up. "Need help getting dressed?"

I gave him what my Daniel would have in similar circumstances.

"I may be old, but I haven't fallen off the perch yet. Give me five minutes, please."

Ford Whitaker, who had returned from Santa Fe that afternoon and joined us for dinner, was explaining how he had been friendly with Shirley, having met her at Weaving Southwest, and had taken her out a couple of times before she met Tony.

"It disappointed me," he admitted, "when she started turning down my invitations and going everywhere with him. I thought he was questionable, a chameleon sort who wasn't much by himself but really turned on the charm with her. When I tried to tell her, she said I was just being jealous and refused to have anything more to do with me."

"Lucky for you," Pat commented.

"Actually unlucky for her, as it turned out," Herrera said.

"How was Alan Medina connected to this?" I wanted to know.

"Medina?" Ford questioned with a frown. "I saw him with Cole several times."

"They had an agreement," Herrera told us. "It was pretty complicated and had nothing to do with either murder— simply a matter of money. Medina is a gambler. He and his gambling buddy have had big debts at the casino out by the pueblo that's run by the Indians—the Red Willow People. He hooked up with Cole and supplied him with paintings to use as pseudo gifts to his current victims in exchange for a cut of the money stolen from them in the con game Cole was running.

"When Cole was killed, Medina hadn't been paid for that last painting Cole had given Shirley. But Medina and his buddy thought it was worth seeing if the con money was still around. If they could find who had it, he thought they might be able to get all of it.

"After Ann's first attempt to kill Shirley didn't work and with her not remembering much, Ann was smart enough to take false credit for saving her tenant and wait to make another try. When Ann convinced him she didn't have the money, Medina thought Shirley might somehow have gotten it back. So they followed her to your motor home, Maxie, then ransacked it in a search for the journal and the money they had decided might be in it."

"How did they know about the journal?"

"By then Ann, who had read parts of it in Shirley's place, had found it was missing as well. She had searched Shirley's things looking for it after killing her because she was afraid there might have been something incriminating written in it at the last that she hadn't seen. She told Medina, so he was looking for it as well. Her mistake was neglecting to take it earlier. I assume she simply forgot."

"And it was in the Winnebago all the time. Was there anything helpful in it?"

"Not a thing. But they took Stretch to see if you could be compelled to turn over either the money or the journal or both."

What confusion. We all sat thinking about it, fitting pieces of the puzzle together in our minds until some kind of picture made sense.

"Seems pretty convoluted to me," Ford said, shaking his head.

Pat nodded. "I know more than I'll ever want to even try to remember," she said.

Butch gave Herrera a searching look, hesitated, then asked the one question that had not been addressed, which I had decided to let slide for my own personal reasons.

"Okay," he said slowly, "I get enough of this to understand most of it, though some of the details and motives are beyond me. But there're two things you haven't told us. Where *is* the money Shirley gave Tony Cole? And who drowned Cole—Jones—whatever his name is—in that vat? I had sort of assumed it must have been Medina."

Herrera shook his head and shrugged.

"I have no idea what happened to the money," he said. "It may be that Cole put it in a bank somewhere under another name and we'll never find it. Hundreds of bank accounts are abandoned by people all the time and never touched again. If he did that, he took its secret to the grave. On the other hand, he may have been carrying the money and whoever killed him may have it."

"And who killed him?"

We all waited while he hesitated, considering.

I held my breath, torn between conflicting emotions, having done my duty and told him all I knew about my midnight visit from Sharon Beil. There was nothing more I could add—except that I had liked and sympathized with the woman and would rather not know that she was responsible. Also, if the money was gone, I would as soon it had gone with her.

Sharon Beil, who had vanished as completely as if she had never existed. And, considering it, I thought I was the only person living who had ever met or talked to her in Taos.

"We found only one set of imperfect fingerprints at the scene that did not belong to the owner," Herrera said carefully. "They might, or might not, be enough to indict someone, but we will not be making an exhaustive search to find that person, who is not a Taos resident and is no longer at the last two known addresses. So we may never know, or be able to prove beyond a reasonable doubt, exactly who killed Earl Jones."

"Well," said Pat, voicing what I'm sure we were all thinking, "he's one less predator loose in the community."

I glanced at Butch and found him looking at me with a pensive expression on his face that disappeared as he smiled and gave me a wink.

"Some strong women around here," he said to Herrera. "At least we've got Maxie back—in good shape if she can just stay out of trouble for a while. So far, every time I meet up with her she's involved in some kind of difficulty."

*"Hey!"* I said. "Who are you to talk?"

"I probably won't be able to get back up here again before you take off," he told me as he was leaving the next afternoon. "But let's keep in touch."

"Absolutely," I promised and meant it. He was, and is, a definite keeper. "I'm thinking of taking the Winnebago to Denver for storage and flying back to Alaska for the summer, but I'll let you know."

"You would probably enjoy being peacefully at home for a while after all this," he said.

"Yes. But I'll stop on my way through Cimarron to see the Tooth of Time, as you suggested."

I stayed another week before leaving Taos, working every day with Pat at Weaving Southwest and learning everything I could about the craft. One afternoon she let me try the large walking loom and I felt that in completing the piece I had begun on my small one I had passed some kind of test.

"You should try tapestry next," she suggested. "At the rate you're going, you'll soon have filled your house with pillow covers."

"There's always Christmas and neighbors to think of."

I had her ship the small loom home to Alaska for me, so it would be waiting when I got there, along with enough yarn to keep me going for the summer. In the fall I intended that Stretch and I would return to claim the Winnebago in Denver and head for somewhere else we'd never been, but I had plenty of time to make up my mind just where that would be.

One evening, remembering the invitation extended by the woman at the Kachina Inn, Bettye Sullivan and I went to watch the Indian dancers from the Taos Pueblo. It was a thoroughly enjoyable performance, with colorful traditional costumes of leather, fabric, and feathers. One woman even had dozens of tiny metal bells that hung from bands around her skirt and made pleasant accompaniment to the recorded drum and chanted rhythms to which seven or eight dancers moved around the circular sand-covered firepit among the trees of the central park area.

I drove out of Taos bright and early on a Monday morning, heading for Colorado again, but this time I was in no hurry, nor was I looking over my shoulder for pursuers, so I stayed overnight again in Cimarron. The next morning I went a few miles south until I reached the Philmont Scout Ranch, where I stopped at the museum and gift shop and asked permission to take a side road that would lead me to a view of the Tooth of Time.

Though I had only meant to take a look and some photographs, the Tooth was an unexpected inspiration and I wound up spending most of the afternoon writing in my journal, as the events of my time in Taos somehow needed to be recorded in a way I could go back to for later consideration. That's part of what journals are for anyway—or at least mine is. It helps me think and reminds me where I have been and what I have learned as a result.

So I wrote down the events, places, and especially the people I didn't want to forget, and the afternoon was old when I laid down my pen, drove back to Cimarron, and took the road north to Raton, where I would cross the Colorado border the next day.

# Twenty-nine

*Twice during the afternoon the woman took the dachshund out for a short walk. The second time, as the shadows lengthened, she used the camera for several shots of the ridge with its distinctive Tooth of Time.*

*Finally, with a sigh, she closed the journal, put it away, and readied the motor home for travel. Turning it around, before starting back along the dirt road, she hesitated and, over her left shoulder, took a long last look at the Tooth of Time, crowning the ridge. Then, satisfied, she nodded and let the Winnebago roll steadily eastward.*

*The breeze had departed in midafternoon. With nothing to lift it, the dust that glowed briefly golden in the long rays of the setting sun drifted slowly back down onto the empty road.*